Billionaire Twin Surgeons

*Worlds collide at the exclusive
Thorncroft Royal Infirmary!*

When a specialist case for a VIP client sees
estranged twins Basilius and Henrik Jansen forced
to work together at the ultraluxurious Thorncroft
Royal Infirmary, tensions reach fever pitch.

But as Bas discovers his one night with stranger
Naomi had consequences, and Rik goes toe-to-toe
with the distractingly beautiful Grace, it's not just
saving lives that has their hearts racing…

Read Bas and Naomi's story,
Shock Baby for the Doctor

And Rik and Grace's story,
Forbidden Nights with the Surgeon

Both available now!

D0728138

Dear Reader,

I can never predict how a story may slide into my brain. Sometimes it's the spark of a scene, perhaps the meet-cute, perhaps the big black moment. Other times it can be the heroine or the hero themselves. In this Billionaire Twin Surgeons duet—my nineteenth and twentieth books!—it was the idea of the twin heroes themselves.

Separated from his brother when they were seven, Basilius "Bas" Jansen has spent most of his life blaming his brother for not backing him up that awful night with their stepfather when they were kids. His brother appearing back in his life is the last thing Bas wants—especially when he's trying to wrap his head around becoming a father himself.

And then there's his heroine, the strong, sexy and fiercely independent Naomi, who is altogether unimpressed with his playboy reputation.

This story was thoroughly enjoyable to write, and I do hope you love both these billionaire twins—and their sassy, fearless heroines—as much as I do.

I love hearing from my readers, so feel free to drop by my site at www.charlotte-hawkes.com or pop over to Facebook or Twitter @chawkesuk.

I can't wait to meet you.

Charlotte x

SHOCK BABY
FOR THE DOCTOR

———

CHARLOTTE HAWKES

HARLEQUIN
MEDICAL
ROMANCE

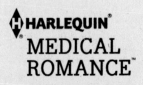

HARLEQUIN®
MEDICAL
ROMANCE™

Recycling programs
for this product may
not exist in your area.

ISBN-13: 978-1-335-40925-6

Shock Baby for the Doctor

Copyright © 2022 by Charlotte Hawkes

For questions and comments about the quality of this book, please contact us at CustomerService@Harlequin.com.

Harlequin Enterprises ULC
22 Adelaide St. West, 41st Floor
Toronto, Ontario M5H 4E3, Canada
www.Harlequin.com

Printed in U.S.A.

Born and raised on the Wirral Peninsula in England, **Charlotte Hawkes** is mom to two intrepid boys who love her to play building block games with them and who object loudly to the amount of time she spends on the computer. When she isn't writing—or building with blocks—she is company director for a small Anglo/French construction firm. Charlotte loves to hear from readers, and you can contact her at her website: charlotte-hawkes.com.

Books by Charlotte Hawkes

Harlequin Medical Romance

Royal Christmas at Seattle General
The Bodyguard's Christmas Proposal

Reunited on the Front Line
Second Chance with His Army Doc
Reawakened by Her Army Major

A Summer in São Paolo
Falling for the Single Dad Surgeon

The Army Doc's Baby Secret
Unwrapping the Neurosurgeon's Heart
Surprise Baby for the Billionaire
The Doctor's One Night to Remember
Reunited with His Long-Lost Nurse
Tempted by Her Convenient Husband

Visit the Author Profile page
at Harlequin.com for more titles.

Mum & Dad

It's nice to be nice… Wait, what the heck do you think you're doing?!

**Praise for
Charlotte Hawkes**

"Wonderful…. Genius…. This author absolutely 100% nailed it!"

—*Harlequin Junkie* on
Reawakened by Her Army Major,
five-star Top Pick!

CHAPTER ONE

BASILIUS JANSEN WASN'T merely aware of his reputation as the incorrigible playboy surgeon of the Thorncroft Royal Infirmary, he actively revelled in his notoriety.

At least, he usually did.

Even now, as he strode purposefully through the corridors towards the resus department, he dipped his head and automatically flashed his trademark killer smile at the usual chorus of flirtatious greetings that rang around every turn.

'Hello, Bas, your surgery last night was amazing.' Hair-twirl.

'Hey, Dr Jansen, have you just been working out?' Sashay.

'Hi, Bas, see you at the Jansen Ball tonight.' Eyelash-flutter.

Smile. Grin. Wink.

But his heart wasn't in it.

It hadn't been for some months now—and these days his greetings were more of a baring of teeth than his usual infamous, wolfish charm. Actually taking any of them up on their overt hints held even less appeal.

He growled under his breath. It made no sense.

Boundary-pushing surgeries, stunning women, and expensive liquor had long been his three favourite activities—in that order. And whilst the latter two had never, *never*, impacted on his medical focus, the phrase 'work hard, party harder' might as well have been coined exclusively for him. And he'd been more than happy with that.

He could blame the letter that lay, even now, crumpled and unread in the bottom of the waste-paper basket—to his mind, sullying the luxuriously appointed corner suite on the coveted twelfth storey of the hospital, which boasted a dual aspect over the verdant green landscape that was Thorncroft Park, and for which he'd worked insanely hard.

It had been the last of three letters that he'd received over the past five months, and though he'd hated himself for even opening it, Bas hadn't been able to stop himself from traitorously skimming the contents.

Henrik—the brother who he hadn't heard from in almost thirty years and would have been happy not to hear from for another thirty years. The brother whose one, all too easily dropped lie had caused their mother to eject Bas from the family home, and turn her back on him, never once responding to a single letter or phone call, from a desperate seven-year-old son.

Learning that Henrik was now a surgeon like him had been galling. Worse, that the man who remained his brother in name only was apparently, not only in Britain, but even now on his way to Thorncroft, already stirring up hateful memories that Bas had thought he'd long-since entombed.

Enkindled, incinerated, and entombed.

And now, apparently, resurrected.

Old, hateful memories rose up shamefully inside him. And Bas hated himself for such weakness. For the fact that a trio of unwanted letters could strip away the happy, shiny life he'd built for himself, and hurtle him straight back in time to his vicious past. Making him wish he were anyone else but himself.

Ludicrous.

Surely he was built to bask in who he was? And revel in his Scandinavian heritage?

From his six-foot-three broad-shouldered frame to his shock of light blond hair, and from the dash of stubble that enhanced his strong, square jawline to his eyes, which were the iciest-blue of the fjords themselves, Bas knew he was heart-stoppingly arresting. Or so women loved to tell him—and who was he to tell them any different?

Yet, as if basking in such heritage wasn't enough, Bas also gloried in his reputation as one of the country's rising plastic surgeons. His name—and indeed that of his even more of a playboy plastic surgeon father—was above the entrance to the *Jansen wing* and it was no coincidence that this ultra-modern, staggeringly hi-tech, private medical suite in Thorncroft Royal Infirmary was one of the most sought-after medical care facilities in the country.

Between his father's high-profile reputation as cosmetic surgeon to the deliriously rich and achingly famous, and his own growing name for plastic surgical trauma, surgeons around the world were fighting for a rotation within one of their three UK-based Jansen facilities.

And now, it seemed, Henrik was to be one of them.

Surely that was reason enough for his own uncharacteristically dour mood?

Yet still, deep down, Bas fought the odd notion that it wasn't just the letter that had got under his skin.

Rather, he was finding it hard to explain the growing sense of disillusionment that had been building inside him for several months now.

Bas couldn't explain it. Or perhaps it was more that he didn't care to. Not for the first time, a memory of the last gala night drifted towards him before he thrust it aside, the way he'd been doing for months.

But sometimes, on nights where sleep eluded him, he caught the distant sound of a big band playing. And he saw a shimmer of emerald, heard the ghost of a sweet laugh, and took in the hint of a delicate scent.

Logic told him the memory wasn't sticking so much because of the woman herself, but more because she'd been a welcome distraction—along with the fact that he'd uncharacteristically tried to drown himself in a bottle of the most expensive brandy he could get his hands on—after receiving

Henrik's first letter. But still, his skull pounded with the effort of keeping the memory at bay.

Bas emitted another low growl and flung the thoughts from his head as he stabbed the buttons to access the main hospital's resus department.

'Someone paged me for a consult?' he announced, striding over to the ward sister, who was standing at the central computer station. 'An eight-year-old who landed face first off a swing?'

'Hey, Bas.' The sister nodded, making a point of flicking her long ponytail as she changed her pose. 'I didn't know you were on call. Lucky us.'

'I could say the same.' He flashed his killer smile again, and she didn't seem to notice how robotic he sounded. Or maybe it was only in his head. 'Which bay did you say?'

She flicked her tongue out over her lower lip—deliberately probably—and lifted her hand to point across the room.

'Bay five.'

Dipping his head in acknowledgement, Bas swivelled on the spot and began to make his way across the floor, relieved to be away though he couldn't explain that, either. Stepping around the curtain to the bay, he took in the sight of an older doctor, Val, who he knew well, smiling at her charge as she carried out her examination.

'I just want a quick feel of your neck, Bradley, can you turn your head for me?'

'Which way?' the kid asked, his voice clearly thick with tears.

'Whichever way you like. That's perfect. Good man.'

Bas watched as Val gently felt the head and neck.

'What have we got?' he murmured to no one in particular, his eyes still on the patient.

'Eight-year-old kid. Bradley,' someone answered. 'He was brought in by paramedics a few hours ago.'

He watched as Val continued to check the kid's head and neck, telling him he was doing great, and asking him to turn his head to the other side.

'Any more details?' Bas pressed, his eyes still not leaving the boy.

'He was playing a game of dare with his friends, trying to see who could swing the highest and then jump off. Bradley fell. We think he landed face first.'

'You only *think* he landed face first?' Bas checked, when they didn't continue.

He turned his head to look, only to find the nurse in question staring at him and blushing bright red.

Great—not what his patient needed.

'Anybody?' he gritted out, barely casting a cursory look at who else was in the bay, waiting to get called on to help Val.

There was another beat of hesitation and then a reluctant voice piped up.

'It seems there were no actual witnesses to the fall. Apparently the other kids had all been distracted when a police car had driven by on the road below the woods, with its blues and twos.'

That voice.

Something walloped into Bas—like being struck by a bullet from a forty-four. Only the impact of this strike was mental as well as physical. He was aware of his head swivelling around though he couldn't have said how he managed to move it.

The flash of green, the laughter, the music, all swirled around his head as he stared at the woman. This time, there was no batting her away from his brain.

Naomi Fox.

The woman who'd been haunting his dreams ever since that night of the gala. Longer, in fact. Because the truth was that he'd noticed her the first day she'd worked on the resus floor—what red-blooded male wouldn't?—but he'd warned himself to stay away.

There had been something about her, something he couldn't quite put his finger on, that had warned him that Naomi Fox was not a woman with whom he could ever share just a simple, single night of harmless fun.

Striking and tall—almost Amazonian—with a halo of shiny black curls that was almost angelic, and a body that was nothing short of sinfully wicked, she was any man's X-rated dream. And even from that one, single case he'd worked on with her, he'd known she prided herself on being serious and professional. Any man chasing her would have to be equally serious.

Which had made her totally off-limits to someone like him. So why was he still staring like some lost puppy?

And still he stared as Naomi blinked, swallowed, and then, inconceivably, carried on. As if she didn't want to acknowledge anything had ever happened between the two of them.

'From what the ambulance crew were able to piece together at the scene, we believe Bradley suffered initial loss of consciousness for a few minutes,' she hurried on. 'He complained of pain to his neck and right side as well as blurred vision when he was admitted. Significant lacerations near the right eye, on the forehead, and to the right side of his upper lip.'

It should feel like a relief that she was pretending to ignore the electricity that positively crackled and arced between them. But it didn't. Not when a myriad questions were tumbling through his traitorous brain, and not when his body was reacting as though he were some kind of excitable adolescent.

Get your head back in the game.

'Do we know what the ground material was?' mused Bas, irritated by how much effort it took him to revert his gaze to the young patient. To concentrate on peering at the boy's facial injuries, and the blood-soaked clothing.

'Possibly a bonded resin rubber mulch.'

'You've taken bloods? Carried out a CT scan?'

Naomi reached to her side and picked up a tablet, walking towards him calmly. Majestically. And he wondered if she knew he'd spotted that faint tremor in her hands.

'Bloodwork was clear, and we did a full body CT.' She handed him the tablet with a set of results. 'It cleared him on any neck or spinal damage, so Val's just taking off the collar to do a final check for where the pain is located. However, scan did show a fracture to the eye socket.'

Hence why he had been called. He watched Val with the boy.

'Great, Bradley, last thing now, can you lift your head off the bed for me, sweetheart?' the doctor was saying. 'Nice. Great work.'

'No internal injuries?' Bas mused.

'We thought possible damaged spleen at first, but that's also come back clear. It's coming down to lacerations to his face, the orbital fracture and the blurred vision.'

'Okay.' He nodded, his eyes still on the scan, before swiping through the rest of the notes. 'I just need a closer look.'

Handing back the tablet, he moved across the space to where Val was finishing up. It should feel like such a relief to step away from Naomi. But it didn't. Not even when it calmed his body down— if only a fraction.

She shouldn't matter to him at all.

'Mind if I take a look, Val?'

'No, of course not.' She blinked at him in surprise. 'Good grief, if it isn't young Basilius.'

They'd known each other so long that it was as if the older woman had released a much-needed pressure valve from the spectre of Naomi, and he cast the older woman a genuine grin.

'Are you ever going to simply call me Bas?'

Val shot him a pointed glance, which had the effect of further helping to ground him. She'd been at Thorncroft for over three decades—a former army nurse who had become a doctor later in life, and whose skills were legendary. But more than that, she was the one new doctors turned to.

She was also the one who had first looked after him when he'd wandered the hospital corridors as a heartbroken child. A desperately confused, lost kid who'd just been foisted onto a father who had never wanted him and who had been—and still was—even more of a Lothario surgeon than Bas.

After twelve months of his being shoved from proverbial pillar to post, his eight-year-old spirit hadn't just been crushed by what had happened with Henrik and their mother, and then his deeply resentful father, it had been utterly decimated.

But then Val had come along, plucking him from whatever unused consultation room or quiet sluice room he'd been hiding in—so that no one could see quite how unwanted he was—and marching him determinedly towards the canteen to feed him up.

And it was Val who had told—instructed—the unapproachable Magnus Jansen that he was going to pay for the refurbishment and redecoration of the small storeroom next to her department, so that Bas would always have a safe space of his own when he was hauled along to the hospital.

Having her there had been better than any babysitter his father could have paid handsomely to employ.

Val had almost been the mother he'd never had.

'I prefer Basilius,' she replied archly, the way she always did. Though the corners of her mouth tugged upwards. 'It is your name, after all, correct? Or perhaps you would prefer the nickname I gave you when you were a boy?'

'No, ma'am.' He laughed. But still, he was entirely too aware of Naomi watching them.

He couldn't shake the feeling that she saw too much. Worse, that he didn't *mind* it.

With a jolt, he turned his attention back to the patient and for the next few minutes Bas busied himself with checking the boy's lacerations, paying particular attention to the right eye socket.

'Good lad, you did well,' he praised the boy at last as he stepped back to where Val was still standing.

But before he could start to speak, she summoned Naomi over. Clearly she was taking the younger nurse under her wing, which meant she thought that Naomi was good. He knew the older woman too well, and it meant she was hoping her young charge would be able to take advantage of the new rules allowing capable nurses to train up as doctors within a matter of a few years.

He tried not to file that away as a point of interest.

'Given the CT results, the location of the fracture, and from what I can see of young Bradley himself, it doesn't look as though he has done damage to the eye itself, or the tear ducts,' he told his old friend.

'That's as I thought.' Val nodded before turning to Naomi. 'But you understand why we paged Plastics rather than suturing ourselves?'

'I do.' To her credit, Naomi looked right at him, even though her voice was quieter than he thought it ought to be. Bas didn't care to examine quite the effect that had on his body. 'Given the complexity of the human face, and Bradley being so young, any doctor who sutures him would need to fully understand the structure beneath, since facial trauma could have such a deleterious effect on the development and growth of facial bones.'

'Good,' Val approved. 'If there was any misalignment of the underlying tissue when they did the suturing, it could result in a malformation, which would likely on become more pronounced as the boy grows up.'

He was about to answer when Naomi started speaking again. More confidently again, this time.

'The fact that the lacerations are in such complex

places—around the eye, on the lip across the ver-
million, and on the forehead—means that particular care will need to be taken to carry out careful
debridement, ensuring no foreign bodies remained,
as well as the suturing itself.'

Clearly, she wanted to learn and he couldn't help
but feel a little impressed. She was like he imagined
a determined young Val to have been.

Only hotter, of course.

And incredibly dangerous to his libido.

'I'm confident I can treat the kid whilst guaran-
teeing little to no scarring,' he heard himself say.

As if he wanted to impress her, too.

He didn't dare glance at Val, and was almost
relieved when a doctor from another bay popped
his head around the curtain and asked if he had a
moment.

But then—with Bradley now occupied by his
mother—it was just him and Naomi, and he wasn't
sure he cared for how much he liked that.

'Okay,' he bit out. 'So, I'll want to carry out a
more detailed test in my own department once Val's
happy to release him but, as I said, at this point it
looks like a minor eye-socket fracture. No suggestion of damage to the tear ducts or eye muscle itself. Most of the time, fractures like this go away
on their own, with application of an icepack, rest,
and pain relief.'

She nodded, then bit her lip and he wondered
how he knew she wanted to ask him a question.

'Go ahead,' he prompted, just as the low buzz of Bradley's mother grew quiet.

So when Naomi murmured quietly, he couldn't quite hear.

He turned to his patient, but the woman was merely kissing her son's forehead, engrossed in pushing the damp, bloodied hair away from his face, even though Val had already ensured it was done.

Still, when Bas turned back he instinctively took a step closer to Naomi, a waft of coconut-scented shampoo assailing his senses.

And this time, the wallop was a hard punch to his gut.

A split-second image of her curls tumbling down onto his chest as she bent her head to kiss a scorching trail along the ridges of the six-pack he was so famous for.

The punch sucked the air from his very lungs.

He'd slept with more than his fair share of women, over the years. But now, looking at Naomi, it was impossible for him to even recall any other name. Or face.

'We considered getting someone from Ophthalmology,' she muttered, and he actually had to fight the urge not to sway closer so that her lips might graze his cheek. 'For the blurred vision.'

Bas hesitated. His throat was suddenly so parched that he could barely breathe. What the heck was happening to him? He enjoyed women, certainly, but they didn't *affect* him. Certainly not like this.

He had no idea how he managed to respond.

'I'll take a closer look upstairs but, at this level, even that often goes away without the need for further treatment,' he ground out. 'I have a case to get back to, but have him sent through when you're finished up.'

'Okay.' Naomi nodded, and something about it sent a whole lot more fragments of memory spiralling through his head.

'Thank you, Basilius.' Val came up behind him.

Bas grunted something akin to a reply as he turned to leave the department. The sooner he got out of here and back to the relative sanctuary of his private wing, the better. He was definitely not accustomed to this sensation of feeling turned inside out.

'Do me a favour, Basilius.' Val stopped him. 'When I send one of my nurses up, don't...shall we say...*keep* her like you did last week.'

Bas turned back, raked his hand through his hair with uncharacteristic irritation. Only Val could get away with addressing him that way, and normally he might have made a joke of it. He was never embarrassed, *ever*, but right now he couldn't even bring himself to look at Naomi.

'Then don't send that nurse again. She seemed to have practically glued her hands to the wheelchair and ended up cluttering up my department for an hour, claiming she needed to wait with the patient. I ended up having to order her out of the wing.'

She had also flirted with him incessantly. Or tried to. He was accustomed to the odd flirtation— or ten—behind the scenes, but this woman had been particularly unprofessional in front of the patient. Something Bas had never tolerated, for all his playboy reputation.

The older woman sniffed tellingly.

'Well, if you didn't play up to that reputation of yours…'

'Val…'

'Fine, I'll have Naomi take him to you.'

'Naomi?' The name rolled around his tongue as if he couldn't help but sample it. Taste it. *Again.*

'Naomi,' Val repeated impatiently, gesturing to his emerald goddess and clearly misinterpreting his hesitation.

Which was preferable to her realising the truth.

'Does she suit your taste better?' she asked, oblivious to the salacious thoughts that promptly raced around his brain. 'She's quiet and professional, keeps herself to herself most of the time, so I can't imagine she'd be the type to be inclined to…*clutter* anywhere up.'

'I'm standing right here,' Naomi spoke up unexpectedly, eliciting a chuckle from Val.

'She also isn't afraid to speak her mind,' Val noted appreciatively. 'Which is why I told your father that he'd better grant her one of your darned prestigious Jansen Bursaries, or I'd want to know why.'

Without knowing he meant to, Bas swung his head back around to peer at Naomi.

'You're a JB recipient?'

'You didn't know?' She narrowed her eyes at him and, too late, he realised he'd almost revealed too much.

Like the fact that, for all that the public reputation of the Jansen brand was that he and Magnus shared a close father-son surgeon connection, the reality was that his father was a prideful, jealous egotist who only acknowledged his own son's achievements because it enhanced the Jansen name and reputation. And, by extension, meant more money flowing in.

The only reason his father offered a handful of bursaries around the country each year, to retrain some of the most promising nurses as doctors, wasn't out of the goodness of his heart, but because the man hoped something so charitable would result in some kind of official honours. Maybe an MBE, or an OBE, but most likely, knowing the ruthless Magnus Jansen as Bas did, he was probably after a knighthood.

Still, less than altruistic motives aside, the Jansen Bursaries were worth their proverbial weight. Usually awarded to kids who had never had the same opportunities to go to university to train as doctors, but who showed particular medical aptitude in whichever medical profession they had chosen instead.

And Naomi Fox was apparently one of them.

'I didn't pay that close attention to who the recipients were,' Bas lied easily, grateful that Val was called away by another doctor just at that moment, and couldn't put her tuppence worth in.

'Of course you didn't,' Naomi clipped out. And there was no reason at all for her disapproval to cut through him the way it did. 'Well, for the record, it was awarded to me a couple of years ago.'

All he could think was that if she'd been awarded the JB a couple of years ago, then she was already part way through her training. So where had she been training up until her move to Thorncroft?

Bas frowned, thinking back to the sparse memos he'd read.

'I thought the new trainee doctor coming to Thorncroft had been an army nurse?'

'That's right,' she confirmed, her tone carefully neutral.

He should have paid more heed to it.

'You?'

Naomi's jaw locked tightly, almost imperceptibly. But Bas didn't miss it. Just as he didn't miss the vaguely defiant tilt of her head. A hint that his magnificent Amazon queen still stalked beneath that calm outer skin.

That image of her, dressed spectacularly in a shimmering emerald sort of metallic dress, hurtled through his mind. And then—more mouth-wateringly—that same dress pooling on the floor of a hotel room, and long, deep brown legs, her feet clad in the sexiest of green heels, stepping seductively out.

And now he found out that his glorious green goddess had been in the army? How deliciously apt.

'You don't think an army nurse could be female?' she gritted out. 'How disappointingly medieval of you.'

'Is it?' he asked, almost cheerfully.

She either didn't know that Val also used to be an army nurse, or she didn't know that *he* knew it. Or perhaps she didn't think he cared enough about his old friend to remember. But instead of setting Naomi right, Bas found himself deliberately goading her and he couldn't seem to help himself. It had to be some twisted reward that when her eyebrows shot up into high, disdainful arches, he found it so utterly fascinating.

'You do know that women have been a part of the British army for centuries, whether it was legal or not?' she demanded.

'Have they really?' He deliberately notched his eyebrows a fraction higher as she glowered at him.

He was getting under her skin and making that professional edge of hers slip—even if only a little. And what did it say about him that he relished the concept?

'Yes. They have,' she hissed. 'In fact, during the

British Civil Wars in the mid-seventeenth century, so many women disguised themselves as male soldiers that Charles I issued a proclamation banning women from wearing men's military uniforms.'

And now he knew he was in even more trouble than he'd first feared. Because, as irrational as it was, he found her waspish attitude all the more thrilling.

It was certainly better than her pretending she didn't know him, that they hadn't spent nowhere near enough glorious hours exploring every single inch of each other's bodies. Indulging in their most carnal needs.

The quiet, almost meek Naomi of before was not the version of her that he wanted to remember.

'Thank you for the impromptu history lesson.' He flashed his most wolfish grin at her. As if he were about to bite her—and probably in the most carnal way—and he revelled in the punch of triumph as she didn't quite suppress a shiver. 'But I'm not entirely ignorant.'

She made a noise that wasn't a grunt precisely, but suggested that she was graciously biting her tongue from verbally expressing her scepticism. No doubt she wouldn't have been so restrained had Val not still been there, though it was getting harder and harder not to forget about the older woman's presence.

'I am fully aware there are plenty of female military nurses, and female military doctors, and, indeed, female frontline combat soldiers,' he told her, his tone deliberately leisurely. 'Val here was also an army nurse, so my surprise was not about females in general—I'm not a philistine—but about *you* in particular.'

'Right.'

She didn't sound as if she remotely believed him, and an inexplicably crazy urge to get under her skin charged through him. He ratcheted his grin up to lethal.

'Especially given that, the night of the gala, you didn't mention being in the military at all. Then again, I don't recall us doing much talking. Do you?'

She made something of a strangled sound, her rich eyes—already the colour of his favourite deep, hickory-infused brandy—darkening to almost black, and her breathing becoming suddenly shallower and more rapid. Clearly their not-even-one-night stand wasn't far from Naomi's mind either.

He didn't know why he should find that so deeply satisfying. Bas grinned.

'I *do* recall asking you to dance, only for you to tell me that my reputation as Thorncroft's playboy of the decade preceded me, and that I should keep on walking.'

Though it hadn't deterred him. Their mutual attraction had been undeniable, and she hadn't tried much to resist him after that. She'd certainly been waiting for him around a quiet corner in the hotel lobby as he'd instructed, when he'd emerged from the gala after her.

'Which is why she's unlikely to be daft enough to fall for your particular brand of welcome party,' Val cut in, reappearing without warning and catching the back end of their conversation as she turned to Naomi. 'You're due off duty in ten minutes anyway, so if you take Bradley up, you won't get collared onto a new case and you might even get home on time, for once.'

If looks could have killed, Bas was fairly sure Val would have been flat out on the floor. Naomi didn't even attempt to conceal her dismay, though he didn't miss the telltale kick of her pulse in her neck.

Right where he was sure he had sampled with great satisfaction, more than once.

It certainly cost him far more than it should have done to bob his head in some semblance of normality as he turned back to the older doctor and forced his suddenly deadweight legs to move again.

'Fine, send her,' he managed, astonished that his voice actually sounded normal. 'She seems perfect.'

Which was not at all what he'd meant to say.

CHAPTER TWO

THIS WAS A NIGHTMARE.

Worse.

Watching a surgeon of Bas's skill suture young Bradley's face with such precision and care deserved to be appreciated. It was like an artform in itself—especially since she'd been interested in this particular speciality ever since she'd been an army nurse and seen the soldiers who could benefit from good plastic surgery.

Certainly, the trainee doctor inside her tried to appreciate Bas's skill. Just as much as the woman inside her tried *not* to appreciate the movement of those muscled biceps, or the defined shoulder blades, as he worked.

She really was losing the plot.

Fighting to stop her hands from moving to her belly in what could too easily be a revealing gesture, Naomi contented herself with scowling around the impressively hi-tech Jansen suite. As though her displeasure could somehow remedy this entire ghastly situation.

How did you tell a one-night stand—not even that long, if she were to be accurate—that you were now expecting his baby?

More significantly, how did you justify *not* telling him?

Obviously, she hadn't expected to be able to stay

out of Bas Jansen's way for ever. To the contrary, she'd known she had to tell him the truth sooner or later. Or, more pertinently, sooner rather than later. It was the right thing to do. The *moral* thing to do. And when he tried to pay her off and buy her silence—which men like him were universally famous for doing—she could tell him quite loftily that she didn't want his money. She didn't want anything from him.

She'd simply be doing the right thing.

There were three problems with that, however. Problem number one was that she had absolutely no idea how she was to begin to go about doing the so-called right thing and telling him the truth.

Especially since—problem number two—to her utter shame she hadn't realised quite how drunk Bas had been until after they'd actually been… intimate. He certainly hadn't shown any…physical signs of liquor-induced impairment—far from it.

And problem number three was that, after looking after herself, her kid sister, and—to a lesser degree—her grandmother ever since she was about fourteen, Naomi was used to dealing with situations all on her own. From cobbling together some kind of dinner—usually a butterless ham or cheese sandwich and a piece of any fruit that Leila might possibly be convinced to eat—when their grandmother was still out at her second job, to racing to her sister's school to try to smooth things over with the irate headteacher when Leila had tried yet another of her pranks.

Naomi had done it all on her own. She simply wasn't accustomed to opening up her life to other people. She wasn't used to baring her heart and *sharing*.

But this was different. This was a baby. And Bas was the father.

And she'd almost told him.

Twice.

The first time had happened the day after she'd spent half the night on the edge of the bath in her tiny, cold apartment bathroom, staring in shock at the white stick in her hand which—for such a little thing—wielded such life-changing power. Bas had stepped into the hospital lift she'd been in. Even though it had been crowded, and even though she'd been half hidden at the back, she'd kept expecting Bas to realise she was there.

But he hadn't.

The second time she'd been throwing herself into her work, grateful for the organised chaos of the resus department to distract her racing thoughts, when, just like today, Bas had strode onto the floor as one of the plastic surgeons on call.

She'd been with a different patient from him but, nonetheless, a part of her had kept expecting him to see her. To stop. To say something. But he'd been wholly focussed on the emergency in front of him, and he hadn't even looked up.

And when he hadn't, it had felt like *fate* lending her a hand and offering her some much-needed space to decide on the best way to proceed, and how she was going to go explaining it all to Bas.

In fact, it had been a shock. She'd known Bas would be in the private Jansen wing where he was paid obscene sums of money for his admittedly formidable skill as a surgeon, but it had come as a shock to realise that he also gave his time to be on call to the main hospital.

It told a story about him that she didn't want to have to factor in to the image of him that she was trying to keep in her head. The image that would make this little pickle she'd got herself into seem easier to bear.

But now, without warning, she found that the sand had run out of her mental hourglass. Bas was right here, in front of her, and there was no way—not morally, anyway—that she could avoid talking to him any longer.

What a mess.

Accepting the Jansen Bursary was supposed to have been a fresh start—that proverbial clean slate. It was her chance to prove to herself, more than anyone else, that she was worthy of first place. That she would never be anybody's second choice, ever again.

And choosing to do this part of her retraining back at Thorncroft—the place where she'd grown up and was, for all intents and purposes, *home*—

was her way of proving to herself that she'd moved on from her less than enjoyable childhood here.

Most of all, retraining as a doctor was supposed to give her the professional life she'd always dreamed of having, but had never thought was for her. Especially not, having effectively taken care of her kid sister, Leila, as well as her grandmother, for most of her life.

It was not, she scowled to herself, supposed to be about falling into bed with the hospital's resident playboy.

And yet, wasn't that pretty much the first thing she'd done?

'Nearly there, Bradley,' she managed to murmur to her young charge, more for something to occupy her mind than out of need.

Bas was doing a flawless job of suturing his patient and talking enough to keep the young boy's mind distracted. He'd even taken the time, whilst anaesthetising the area, to discover his young patient's interests, so that he could keep his conversation light and relevant.

He wasn't just an impressive surgeon, he actually cared about his patients, too.

Damn Bas Jansen and the stupid bursary. Did she really believe that she might lose her one chance at becoming a doctor if he found out her secret? Had she really feared that he might take her bursary away as some sort of revenge?

Or was it more that she feared her own reactions?

And the fact that losing her prized bursary would be another reason to look at herself as second-rate.

Certainly, the most incriminating part about the unexpected earlier encounter was that heat, that awareness, still simmered between them.

The *need*.

And not for someone stable, and kind, and potential partner material, but for the kind of playboy male that she'd sworn she would never be foolish enough to fall for. If she'd learned anything from her absent mother, surely it had been that much?

She waited until he finished up, with more words of praise for his patient before turning to her.

'Wait here with young Bradley whilst I go and speak to his parents,' he instructed as he peeled off his surgical gloves.

Without waiting for an answer, he was gone and finally, *finally*, Naomi felt as though she could breathe.

'Well done, Bradley, you did really well.' She smiled brightly as she crossed the room to him. 'Dr Jansen just wants a quick word with your parents and then they'll be in here to sit with you a little longer, whilst we discharge you.'

Which meant she could get back downstairs, out of the private wing that was Bas's territory, and to the relative safety of the main hospital. And if that made her a coward, then so be it.

Still, she wasn't entirely prepared when the door opened a few minutes later as Bas held it open for the parents to enter and signalled her out, making her stomach lurch horribly.

At least, she told herself it was 'horribly'. It couldn't possibly be in anticipation.

'I should accompany the family out,' she managed as he closed the door behind them, leaving the two of them alone in the sleek corridor.

'Give them a bit of time to catch their collective breaths.' Bas strode down the hallway, leaving her standing outside the door.

Without stopping, he half turned to call over his shoulder.

'Let's go, Fox.'

What did it say that her legs followed, almost of their own volition?

'Don't call me that,' she muttered as she caught up to him.

'What? *Fox?*' She didn't need to see his face to hear that grin of his. The one that was all straight white teeth, which she could practically feel against her skin. 'It's your name, isn't it?'

She couldn't bring herself to answer. At least it was better than *älskling.* He'd called her that that night. It had sounded far too intimate, and made her feel things she ought not to have felt.

'Isn't that how you guys address each other in the army?' he challenged, his cheerful tone mercifully dragging her back to the present.

'Sometimes.' She gritted her teeth, and tried to shoot him a dirty look. 'But you are not them.'

Not least because no one else could infuse it with quite the same sense of wicked delight as Bas could.

Or perhaps that said more about her than she wanted to admit right now.

And still, she was obediently following him through the pristine wide corridors, without demanding where he was leading her.

'I hadn't expected to see you in the main hospital,' she managed, at last.

'Indeed?'

'I figured you spent all your days up here, in the Jansen wing.'

He stopped and eyed her.

'You mean in my ivory tower that is a private suite?' he asked, a little too perceptively.

She wrinkled her nose, not liking how easily he seemed to be able to read her. Again.

'Perhaps I would have stayed up here.' He lifted his hand in a gesture that might well have been a shrug. 'But you paged me.'

He had a point. More accurately, though, Bas hadn't been on call. The moment Val had realised that the plastics surgeon who was on call was already with an emergency, she'd told Naomi to page up to the private suite. She'd known Bas would send someone if he could.

Actually, the older doctor had offered quite a few surprisingly complimentary insights into Bas, the surgeon. Not that Naomi was about to mention any of them.

'I did not page...*you*,' she emphasised instead. 'I paged someone from your department. I thought you might send someone else. Someone more junior.'

'Then it was your lucky day, or rather your patient's lucky day, since I was free.' He levelled his gaze at her. 'Or would your patient have preferred someone more...junior?'

Naomi cast him another dirty look, and he didn't care to evaluate what it meant that he got a kick out of getting a rise out of her.

'Obviously not,' she gritted out, before emphasising, 'My *patient* will be better with the best he can get.'

'I'm flattered.' He laughed.

She scrunched up her nose.

'Don't be.'

But apparently he wanted to needle her some more.

'Perhaps you should refrain from calling me the next time some kid inconveniently falls from a playground swing and smashes his face. I would, of course, far rather be in the ivory tower than down here in the dirt.'

Heat bloomed in her cheeks. Still, she wasn't about to apologise outright, it seemed.

'All right, no need to be facetious,' she muttered. 'I now know you're a dedicated surgeon, especially for patients who really need your help, whether they're private patients or not.'

'How very magnanimous of you,' he remarked dryly.

But, as his eyes locked with hers, another jolt of electricity arced between them, and she couldn't respond. With one look, he'd sent her mind spinning, and spinning, and threatening to upend everything she knew to be logical.

What was she thinking, goading this particular man? Not just a fellow colleague to whom she ought to show respect, for his surgical ability if no other reason. Not simply a member of the hospital board who could have her fired for talking to him in such a way, if he so chose—not that she thought he would. But as the man who was, for better or for worse, the father of the unborn baby she was currently carrying.

A result of the one and only one-night stand she'd ever had in her entire life.

She was almost surprised he hadn't noticed. The bump wasn't huge, but it was clearly there. Then again, the flowing tops she'd taken to wearing recently helped. Along with the fact that she had become adept at keeping the patient between her and other staff, and if not the patient themselves, then a piece of medical equipment. The bed, the monitoring equipment, a computer, it didn't matter what.

Anything to keep off the hospital grapevine for as long as she possibly could. The last thing she wanted was to be the gossip of the whole of Thorn-croft Royal Infirmary. Hadn't she had enough of that throughout her entire childhood?

She'd grown up standing out from the crowd. With people staring at her. Talking about her. Because of her family situation, with both parents absent, her height, making her eight-year-old self look like a twelve-year-old, and her skin colour, which didn't match her own mother or grandmother, let alone anyone else on the estate.

She didn't know how long they stood there. Perhaps a few seconds, perhaps a few lifetimes. There were mere inches separating them, though it might as well have been a gaping chasm, and yet at some point, she realised, she'd clenched her fists in her pockets. Presumably in some desperate attempt to stop herself from reaching out. Reaching *for* him.

It didn't help that he was staring back at her with such an expression tugging at his unaccountably striking features. As though he was reliving the same memories. As though he still wanted her, too. Every bit as badly as she wanted him.

But that couldn't be right.

The entire hospital knew that Bas Jansen didn't do revisits. She was simply projecting her own silly fantasies onto him.

And she still needed to tell him the truth. Now. Before she bottled out yet again.

It wasn't as though she needed him to respond. In truth, she doubted he would be remotely pleased to hear what she had to say, and he'd be more than happy to hear that she didn't expect him to play any kind of active role.

But still, she had to do the honourable thing and at least...*tell* him the truth. She might have spent the past few months telling herself that *not* telling him was the right thing to do—the honourable one.

Now, she feared, it had just been the cowardly thing to do. And she was nothing if not a person who owned her mistakes.

'Bas...' she choked his name out '... I have to talk to...'

'Not here,' he rumbled, his voice low.

Without warning, he lifted his finger and pressed it gently to her lips. A jolt of electricity fired through her in an instant, leaving her body tingling crazily whilst her brain turned to mush.

She might have thought it embarrassing had she been able to think at all.

A thousand warning sirens going off in her head at once. Accompanied by a thousand brightly lit fireworks. The part of herself that wanted him—so very badly—warring with the part of herself that hated such weakness.

And so, her eyes were riveted on him. Then, abruptly, Bas spun away and resumed his striding through the corridors, leaving her hurrying to keep up.

Or be left behind altogether.

'Where are we going?' she muttered as she raced

after him, his long, muscled legs eating up the long, pristine corridors.

'Patience,' he told her airily. Or perhaps it was *patients*.

She couldn't stop herself from asking him.

'Both, *älskling*.'

And there was that endearment again.

She panicked as he flashed her his trademark grin—the one that usually had an assortment of women falling over themselves.

All she could do was roll her eyes. It was that, or swoon. And she refused to let him see her do the latter.

But Bas didn't notice. He was already a few feet ahead of her.

She'd never felt so glad to be able to keep up with him without needing to break into a run; odd, since she'd spent most of her life hating being tall—yet another difference making her stand out from most other girls.

Being a nurse in the army had been somewhat better. Her colleagues and senior officers had been more interested in whether she could help save lives or not. Coming back to Thorncroft had only happened because her sister had started playing up again. This time more rebellious than ever. And her grandmother was getting too old to control an ever more wilful teenager.

Still, it had shocked them all when it had worked. With her sister back around, Leila had knuckled down and had just secured a place on a fashion course at the college just outside Thorncroft. And her sister was like a different girl, the happiest and most settled that Naomi thought she'd ever seen her. So, in that respect, opting to give up her career in the army had been worth it.

By contrast, ending up pregnant with the child of her benefactor's son certainly hadn't been part of Naomi's big plan. Not least because she'd never wanted to emulate the mother she'd barely ever known.

She'd thought it couldn't get much worse…until Bas had walked into Bradley's bay in the resus department, and it had been as though her entire body had ignited all at the same time.

There had been no denying it, even in that first moment that he'd rounded the curtain. The chemistry from that night had been there, swirling around the vast space and shrinking it to a tenth of its size.

Smaller, even.

When he'd turned to look at her, she'd feared the closeness might suffocate her. Or perhaps it had been more like the memory that had clawed through her. The *need*.

With every hair on her arms, her neck, standing to attention.

She'd known seeing him again wouldn't be easy, but she'd never imagined it would be *this* hard. And that was without even telling him that she was expecting his baby.

Naomi's stomach lurched horribly.

However many times she'd run through the scenario in her head these past few months, she still hadn't worked out the best way to give a person that kind of news. It was the excuse she'd been giving herself for not having sought him out before now. It had been hard enough to work out how to approach it, and that had been before it had become apparent that the chemistry still fizzed.

But now he was here, scant inches away. And she couldn't fake any more excuses. She *had* to tell him.

'Bas—'

'Ready?' he cut her off cheerfully.

'Ready for what? No, wait…'

But it was too late, he was already opening the door and stepping inside. All she could do was follow.

'Hey, Jimi, Heather, how are you doing this afternoon?'

A young boy, perhaps mid-teens, looked up from the comic book he was reading, a genuine smile brightening what had been a rather sullen expression.

'Hi, Bas.'

It was echoed by a woman, clearly his mother, who was sitting in a chair across the room, also reading quietly. The woman looked tired but welcoming, and Naomi shot her an easy smile, before joining Bas at the young boy's bedside.

'This is Naomi Fox—I mentioned her before, you remember? She's a junior doctor who is interested in my field of work.'

'Hi, Jimi.' Naomi smiled softly, stepping forward to shake the boy's hand. But thoughts were racing through her head at a hundred miles per hour.

When had Bas talked to this boy? Presumably when he'd left the resus department ahead of her. And had he really remembered that she'd been interested in his specialism? It was something she'd mentioned briefly, the night of the gala, but Bas had been more interested in other things than conversation that night.

Then again, so had she.

'Hi,' the boy managed tightly, barely looking her in the eye. He pulled the bed covers up over his chest awkwardly.

'Nice name, huh?' Bas stage-whispered.

'Nice,' Jimi mumbled, flushing a deep scarlet, though it was clear to Naomi that he delighted in the camaraderie with Bas.

'I've been telling him that you were a nurse in the army.' Bas turned to her, before swinging back to his patient. 'Jimi is hoping to join as a vet, one day. Right, buddy?'

'Yeah.' The boy wrinkled his nose and forced himself to relax his white-knuckle grip on the fabric. 'As long as the doc here can fix me.'

Naomi glanced at Bas, smoothing her uncertainty into a mask.

'Jimi, can I carry on? And remember, if you've changed your mind about talking to Naomi, that's fine.'

The boy pulled a pained face, but shook his head.

'No, I…want to.' His fingers moved to his pyjama shirt. 'Should I…?'

'If you're ready, buddy.' Bas nodded, turning back to Naomi, his voice deliberately professional. 'Jimi came to me about a year ago suffering from idiopathic unilateral gynaecomastia as a result of pubertal development.'

Naomi watched as Jimi finished unbuttoning his shirt and, after a quick glance at his mother for reassurance, he opened it for her to see.

One side presented as a flat, boy's chest, the other presented like a clear female breast.

'So, then, there's no way to know why this has happened?'

'The major cause of gynaecomastia is considered to be an imbalance between oestrogen and androgen effects, largely as a result of an over-increase in oestrogen production. But in cases like Jimi's, where it only affects one side, that provides an additional layer of complication.'

'Right.' She bobbed her head in understanding. She had so many more questions, but not all of them would be suitable to ask in front of the patient himself.

'As you can see, it's quite large,' Bas noted. 'And although in Jimi's case the mass is benign, it has understandably had a significant negative impact on his self-esteem, affecting all aspects of his life, not least his schooling.'

'I can't do PE in school, or go swimming,' Jimi muttered. 'I get laughed at, or called Jemima instead of Jimi. They tell me to show them my…'

He tailed off, clearly embarrassed, and Naomi's heart went out to him.

'His schoolwork began to suffer and it began to really damage his relationship with his mum, because of their frequent rows over missing school, or playing truant.'

'Constant rows,' Heather offered sadly. 'Though I can't imagine how it was for Jimi, putting up with those boys. And girls, too, sometimes.'

'Kids can be horribly cruel,' Naomi agreed. Wishing she knew the right thing to say. 'I can sympathise, Jimi, I had my own share of idiot bullies, too. I admire how brave and mature you clearly are, Jimi.'

He glanced at her almost hopefully.

'You think so?'

'I do.' She nodded, relieved.

'Hey, buddy,' Bas teased gently. 'Your mum and I have been telling you that for months, and you didn't believe us? But when a pretty doc tells you, you believe her?'

The boy grinned and flushed scarlet again.

And as crazy as it was, and as much as she knew Bas had simply been using her to strengthen his connection with the young boy, when Bas lifted his head to share a warm glance with her, Naomi had to fight to pretend that her own body wasn't sluiced with heat.

'So.' Bas turned his focus back to his patient. 'Jimi has been through both physical and psychological evaluations to ensure that surgery is for him—I think it's fair to say quite a few psychological evaluations, wouldn't you, Heather?'

'A ton of them,' the mother agreed emotionally. 'Though I'm grateful for every single one of them now that they've finally brought us to this point.'

'But Monday's the big day, right, Bas?' Jimi looked simultaneously eager and emotional.

'It is indeed.' Bas lifted his arm for a fist bump, which the young boy was only too happy to provide.

It was impossible not to smile.

Her own worries seemed so insignificant compared to what this boy was going through. And it was clear that none of the claims she'd heard—that the gifted Bas genuinely cared for his patients—were exaggerated.

All of which might not erase the concerns she had about telling him the truth about her own current situation, but at least they reinforced her belief that telling him was the right thing to do.

Whatever he chose to do—or not to do—about it.

'Thank you so much for trusting me enough to

show me, Jimi.' She focussed on the young boy with a positive smile.

'After Monday, I won't have anything to show anyone any more.'

'It's important to remember that, although I'll use every trick I know to minimise the scarring, there will still be some,' Bas noted carefully, and Naomi knew he was ensuring he managed the boy's expectations.

'I know.' Jimi nodded at once. 'But a scar will be sick. Like a battle wound. Not like—'

'Everyone will say how cool it will be,' Heather jumped in.

Jimi rolled his eyes.

'*Sick*, Mum,' he groaned. 'It'll be sick. Not cool.'

'Yeah, buddy, you'll be sick.' Bas grinned. 'Okay, I'm going to leave you to educate your mum on current vernacular.'

'Okay, see you, Bas.'

'Bye, Jimi. Heather,' Naomi added as she followed Bas out of the door.

She waited until they were in the hallway before talking again.

'He must have been getting a really hard time with other kids.'

'I think it's safe to say that the last few years have been hell for him,' Bas agreed. 'Plastic surgery for kids can be quite controversial but I've performed thousands of similar operations—though not all gynaecomastia—over the years, and it never fails to get me, how much difference it makes to their lives.'

'Do the other kids really let them forget it?' she couldn't help asking.

'Definitely. There's always one kid who wants to keep it alive, but it's incredible how quickly most other kids forget, and life goes back to normal for my patient, once all traces of the disfigurement are gone. I thought you might like to see it for yourself, given your interest.'

She bit her lip, weighing up whether to refer to that night together, or not. She almost didn't, but she was going to have to mention it at some point, so why not in this context?

'I was surprised you remembered our conversation. I didn't think... I thought you hadn't really been interested.' She stopped awkwardly.

'Remembered what conversation?' And it had to be her imagination that made it seem as though he was staring at her with such an intensity. 'I read it in your application file.'

She swallowed once. Twice.

'Bas, I...'

'Wait,' he instructed in a low voice, before turning back up the corridor and summoning her to follow.

He had a point. As quiet as these private wing hallways seemed to be, there could easily be someone around the corner, standing by an open door.

Sucking in a breath, Naomi tucked her hands

into her pockets and concentrated on keeping pace with him. Again. She just had to hold her nerve a little longer, but it wasn't easy when, with every step, she felt as though the knot inside her were pulling tighter and tighter.

The memories.

The last time they'd been stalking halls together, it had been in a hotel rather than a hospital. Her hand had been enveloped in his and they'd been hurrying towards a luxury suite, having escaped the gala as it had been in full flow several floors below.

And she had to wonder what it was about Bas Jensen that had her obeying in a way she never would have obeyed any other man.

What was it about Bas that seemed to wind its way right through her—and, given her current situation, how was she ever to break the effect?

CHAPTER THREE

THE WORST THING about it all, Naomi decided a few moments later, was that Bas had a way of making everything feel so thrilling and dangerous, and yet so much fun.

Even now, the thrall that she remembered from the night of the gala spiralled up inside her again, and that familiar heat threatened to spill out of her. Enough to make her keep overlooking the uncomfortable truth that she should have told him a few months ago.

But having the full attention of Bas Jansen was a heady experience, and everything about him that night had been raw, and edgy. And now, just like then, her thoughts were fuzzy in her brain as he had her feeling white-hot and so, so bright, like nothing she'd ever known before. As if she were molten everywhere.

Everywhere.

She could remember her heels sinking so deep into the plush pile of the hotel corridor. And the way her dress—a pretty enough green thing that she'd found in a charity shop, but which Leila had taken and worked her incredible magic on—had moulded itself so lovingly to her body, making her actually feel sexy as she'd hurried along.

Now she was in trainers and scrubs. But some-

how that same thrill—that same anticipation—
seemed to be winding its way through her.

It was insane.

But she wasn't the same woman she'd been a few
months ago—four and a half months, if she was
going to be precise—and that was a fact she simply had to hold on to.

'In here,' Bas gritted out, stopping so suddenly
that she practically turned ninety degrees on the
spot to obey without cannoning into him.

And then she followed him into his office.

It was the view that struck her initially. An incredible view of Thorncroft through two stunning
windows set perpendicular to each other, giving
the impression that the viewer was master of it all.
And perhaps, in Bas's case, that was true.

The Jansen name was more than just *well known*
in these parts. It was positively lauded. And it was
a reminder that she didn't run in remotely the same
circles as Basilius Jansen.

But still, she couldn't stop herself.

'Wow.' She exhaled deeply, her legs moving her
across the room, until she was right in front of that
incredible view, her hands braced on the thin edge
of metal that offered an internal barrier. 'People
would pay good money for this view.'

'I didn't bring you here to look at the view,
älskling.'

His voice rolled through her like another crack
of thunder, reminding her that this wasn't the rea-

son she had come here, either. Slowly, almost against her will, she turned around.

Then wished she hadn't as every single thought poured out of her head, as she became acutely aware that they were entirely alone for the first time since the gala night. And Bas was advancing on her. As if she'd brought him her dues and he'd come to collect.

Naomi wasn't sure she was still breathing.

His eyes were almost black with desire, foolishly daring her to believe that perhaps that gave her some power in this little scenario, even when her brain was telling her it knew better. Whilst all she could do was simply stand there, her heart unable to decide whether it was lurching or stuttering, as though she was *waiting* for him.

And then he was bending his head to brush her lips with his, but even though she lifted her hands to his chest to push him away, she found instead that they shamelessly flattened themselves in surrender against the hard wall of muscles that she could still remember tasting.

Instantly, Bas closed the rest of the gap and skilfully claimed her mouth with his own. And, just like that fateful night, it was enough to turn her inside out, tumbling and twisting as she plummeted right back into his particular brand of rabbit hole.

She certainly wasn't prepared for him to jerk back from her, his eyes searching hers as though looking for some kind of answer. Or for him to mutter so low under his breath that she couldn't quite make out the words, which sounded like, 'It's all come back to me, now.'

For an achingly long moment, neither of them moved. And then Bas took a step backwards.

'I thought you might like to join me for Jimi's operation,' he murmured, as though it was the most seductive offer in the word. And, in a way, it was. 'Watch it. Learn from it.'

She ought to accept. It was an incredible offer; would-be surgeons fought tooth and nail for such an opportunity. So who cared if he was giving her the opportunity because of this wild chemistry, fizzing between them?

Who cared what had just happened—and not happened—between them?

She ought to be leaping at the chance, but instead her own secret weighed on her too heavily. Naomi opened her mouth only to find she couldn't even speak.

He cocked his head as though assessing her thoughtfully. And he shifted, as if mentally moving past whatever had just struck him a moment ago. Back to the cool controlled Bas for whom Thorncroft was so famous.

'Suddenly coy, Naomi?' he demanded. 'I don't recall you having any such qualms the night of the gala. Wasn't that the bargain you drove with me? I asked for a dance, and you said you'd only agree if I promised to walk you through one of my patient cases? That my field of expertise was what had originally attracted you to medicine. Though you cleverly failed to add that you were retraining as a doctor. And certainly not that you were a recipient of my father's Jansen Bursary.'

'I'm surprised you remember,' she quipped, before she could help herself.

The truth was, she had barely recalled that conversation herself. She hadn't felt like herself from the moment he'd begun to weave his very unique variety of magic.

He laughed, and she felt it. Intimately.

'Most women want something else from me than letting them in on a medical case.'

'I'd have thought there were so many women in your life that you couldn't really keep track.'

'Is that really what you think?' he challenged, in a surprisingly cheerful tone, all things considered. 'Only that hardly reflects well on you either, if that's your opinion of me.'

Her mouth seemed terribly parched, all of a sudden.

'Why, because I slept with you?'

And when he grinned at her like that—his teeth bared so sharply that she could practically feel them against her bare flesh—it only sent another delicious, if uninvited, shiver skimming down her spine.

God, how was it possible that she still wanted him so badly?

No, *craved* him.

And then he spoke and made it ten times worse.

'I don't recall much *sleeping* going on.'

No. Neither did she, if she was truly honest. Though that hour with Bas had been the most reckless, most thrilling, hour of her life.

It had also been the most life-changing, which only made her hate herself even more for showing such weakness as to fall for it again now.

Just like her mother with any one of the scores of insanely beautiful, but utterly unreliable men in her life.

Naomi shook her head as if hoping that could dislodge the unwelcome thought.

'No?' he asked, apparently deciding the head-shake was for him.

What did she say now? A thousand thoughts chased through her.

'*No* as in you agree not much sleeping went on? Or *no* as in you're claiming you don't remember?'

'*No* as in I don't remember.' She seized on the excuse instantly, realising too late that was exactly what he'd expected her to do.

He hadn't been throwing her a lifeline. He'd been laying a trap.

And she'd stumbled straight into it.

'How disappointing.' His eyes gleamed wickedly. 'Then, allow me to remind you.'

Before she could react, he had closed the gap again, and even as she backed up she managed less than a foot before the wall stopped her. There was nowhere to go.

And a part of her thrilled at the notion.

Tilting her head up, her body no longer remembering to even breathe, Naomi felt her traitorous eyelids flutter closed as her lips parted in anticipation. She didn't need to see him to know Bas's head was inching lower, then lower again. And this time, she had time to think how his breath skimmed her cheek, warm and minty—a far cry from the rich, smoky brandy taste of his mouth from that first night—but then…he stopped.

Again.

He was still there. She was so aware of him, she could sense exactly how he loomed over her—making her palms literally itch with the effort of not reaching out and laying them on that impressive chest of his. Not reacquainting herself with every mouth-watering millimetre of the granite wall.

It took her far too long to realise that the kiss hadn't happened. And even longer to sluggishly open her eyes.

He drew his head back slowly, his mouth spreading into yet another broad smile, and his head cocked at a jaunty angle. The bastard was teasing her.

'What,' she managed, 'was that about?'

'I was giving you chance to object,' he told her cheerily. 'To tell me that you didn't want reminding. I find it interesting how remarkably silent you were on the matter, however.'

She fought to regroup, though she noted that neither of them moved.

He was right. She hadn't said a word because she wanted this. She wanted him to kiss her again. Just one more precious memory to lock away—as pathetic as that was—before she told him the truth, and then watched him run for the hills. Or, more aptly, ejected her from his private, hi-tech Jansen suite.

'I didn't see the point in objecting,' she told him primly—or what she'd intended to sound prim. 'You're Basilius Jansen. You do exactly as you please.'

'Not like that, I don't.' He didn't sound offended, exactly. More…firm. 'Not if the woman doesn't want it, too.'

Yet before she could register what was happening, he'd taken a step back. And what did it say about her that every last inch of her body decried the loss?

'Do you get many women who don't want to?' she heard herself ask, in a voice that was too sharp for her liking. 'To that end, do you get *any*?'

He lifted one sculpted shoulder, which his shirt and tailored waistcoat did nothing to disguise—quite the opposite.

'All the more reason for me not to do exactly as I please.'

He didn't say anything more. He didn't need to. Eventually, she gritted her teeth and blew out a deep breath.

'All right; not like that,' she agreed. 'Why would you need to, when you've got practically half the hospital—half the county—falling over their feet for the chance to spend a night with you?'

'A mild exaggeration.' He arched an eyebrow, but at least he didn't seem so stern. 'I seem to recall that you chose not to remain the whole night in my hotel room.'

She hadn't thought she could.

'You sneaked out when I was in the shower,' he continued. 'When you could have joined me instead and continued our exploration of each other.'

'I didn't…'

Naomi tailed off. She hadn't realised that was an option, and whilst the logical part of her wanted to say she would have left anyway, the foolish side of her brain couldn't help feeling that she'd somehow short-changed herself.

Another weakness to hate herself for.

'Besides,' Bas cut in mildly, 'I'm not interested in the rest of the hospital, right now. I'm interested in you.'

'*Interested?*' she heard herself echo weakly.

It struck her that she so desperately wanted to believe him. But she had to keep focussed on those two telltale words he'd uttered…that he wasn't interested in anyone else *right now*.

And she still hadn't told him what she ought to have.

She snaked out a tongue to moisten her suddenly parched lips, only realising her mistake when his eyes dropped to watch the movement.

'I can read women, Naomi.' His voice was too gravelly for her to think straight.

Almost as if he was fighting himself just as much as she was fighting herself.

'You can?' she managed.

'Oh, I can,' he assured her. 'And I know you want this, too. But if you want to pretend that you don't…then I'm definitely not about to force you to admit the truth.'

To her shame, she felt as if she had to fight her body not to simply offer itself up to him to do with exactly as he pleased.

'I… I thought you didn't sleep with the same woman twice?' She barely recognised her own voice. It sounded too thready, and wanton.

But she wasn't here for this. She was here to tell him…what was she here to tell him, again?

'I don't,' he growled. 'But then, I hardly count that brief interlude between us as a full experience, as good as the sex was. My dates usually stay the entire night, at least. As a result, I find my appetite for you has been whetted…but by no means satisfied.'

His words thrilled and prodded her in equal measure. He might want a fuller experience, but it was somewhat embarrassing to admit that the so-called 'brief interlude' with Bas had been the most incredible, intense sex she'd ever had.

She didn't know she'd meant to move until she'd taken a step towards him.

'The rumours...' she began, trailing off as he stretched his arms out until his hands were clamped around her shoulders.

But instead of pulling her in, he held her there. Until the urge to topple against him almost overwhelmed her.

'I can't say I've ever really cared for rumours,' he grated out. 'But maybe there is some truth in them.'

'Oh,' she managed, flicking her tongue out again. He watched that, too.

'Though, since you're here—' how was it possible for a voice to scrape through her with such longing whilst simultaneously demanding of her? '—perhaps I can make an exception. For you.'

Later, much later, she would think it was that last part that ultimately undid her. The idea that he was going against his own unspoken rules just because it was her.

It was a spell that proved too bewitching to undo.

'Unless there is any reason you can think why we shouldn't?' he prompted, his voice still low, now sending her heart into a reckless thumping.

There is a reason, a part of her brain roared at her. But as though from behind inches-thick glass. Too muffled to make out properly.

'No reason,' she heard herself whisper. 'But…'

'I like the first part of that answer best,' he growled. 'So either walk out of here now, or accept the consequences.'

Another warning bell went off in the back of her mind, but she just couldn't focus.

Everything was spinning too fast, and she couldn't find anything to reach out and grab, in an effort to steady herself. To say something. Anything.

Then, before she could think any more, Bas's mouth slammed into hers, claiming her, and everything went too bright. It was as if a part of her had been lost ever since the morning she'd left his hotel suite.

And this time, mercifully, she didn't think he was going to stop it.

There have to be a hundred reasons not to do this, Bas thought dimly as he claimed Naomi's mouth with his for the second time. But for the life of him—as she moulded her body to his as though she had been handcrafted to fit him—he couldn't think of a single one.

It was as though this moment had been inevitable, right from the moment she'd come up to the Jansen wing. From the moment he'd walked onto that resus floor. From even before that.

There was a good reason for his reputation for

never revisiting previous lovers. He had never even been remotely tempted to break that rule. Until *her*.

But the difference was, he hadn't even remembered her until today—though he didn't know how the hell that was even possible. How he could have forgotten a woman like Naomi, even for an instant.

He'd remembered the dress. And the sound of her laugh. Even the scent of her shampoo. But he hadn't remembered *her*. Not the way she deserved to be remembered. *Revered*.

But one kiss—one simple brush of his lips over hers—and it all come crashing back. His memory, like the swell of a wave forming behind him, and then breaking over him. He'd been drinking far too much that night—trying to send the letter from Henrik into oblivion—and then she'd appeared at the bar beside him.

Even her sensual, slightly husky voice asking the bartender for a simple spritzer had slid into his head, and then down to his sex. As provocative as if she'd just stroked right along its length.

When had any woman ever made him feel so winded? As though he'd been burning straight through for her, and the longer they'd fought each other, the higher the flames had licked.

And there had been far too many other things he would rather have been licking, right then.

Just as he would now.

Because as fast as he was losing his fight to resist Naomi Fox, his consolation was that she was losing her battle to resist him, even faster.

He could certainly use the fact that she wanted him—*this*—to his advantage. Anything to make him feel less…*savage.*

Angry at her for walking out of his hotel room that night, instead of staying. Even angrier at himself for having let her. If he hadn't been dashing for the shower in an attempt to clear the uncharacteristic fuzziness from his head—purely so that he could appreciate her properly—then he surely wouldn't have been so stupid as to leave her alone. To leave her in any doubt that he wanted her to join him.

It was true what he'd said to her earlier about that brief interlude having whetted his appetite but not satisfied it. Surely that was the reason she'd been haunting his head these past months.

Naomi Fox was the reason why he'd recently lost his stomach for women and drink. The reason that only surgeries seemed to hold his attention these days.

He was still hungry for her, and once he'd sated that need—once he had taken a long, indulgent night getting to know every inch of her glorious body—he could shake off this odd melancholy that had taken hold of him, and he could get back to his easy life, be his playboy surgeon self.

Business as usual. Simple.

Bas ignored the niggling voice in his head that contemplated otherwise.

He wasn't interested in arguments, or deep thought. He was only interested in the here and now. In the way that Naomi was pressed so tightly against him—every inch of their bodies craving the contact. He wasn't quite sure when his hands had managed to sneak under the tunic of her uniform, but somehow they were splayed widely over her stomach and waist. If he was to inch them a fraction higher, they would skim the curve under her breast, and he knew from experience how she would react.

He didn't know how he held himself back from doing so.

All he could concentrate on was the feel of her mouth under his lips. The way her indecently sensual lips parted so sweetly, opening up to him. Inviting him in. And all he could do was kiss her, again and again, as if he couldn't get enough. As if he'd never be able to get enough.

For the first time, he was beginning to know what it must feel like to be addicted to something. To feel that helpless, yet that invigorated, all at once. Everything about her seemed to enslave him.

He didn't care to analyse what shot through him at that.

Instead, Bas busied himself with kissing her. Sampling her. Over and over again. He moved one hand to cup her cheek, his fingers sliding through that abundance of thick, bouncy curls, tilting her head to the side and angling her mouth for a tighter fit.

It was a revelation, the way her tongue swept against his. How had he forgotten the thrill that had given him, that first night together? How had he forgotten the thrill that was Naomi?

He'd thought he'd remembered. He'd thought he'd replayed every last second of it—despite his attempts to censor his brain—innumerable times over the past few months. But not one of his thrilling vivid recollections had come close to capturing every last detail of being with her.

That fact alone should strike fear into his very core.

Sliding his hands over her velvet-soft skin, both exploring and reacquainting, Bas cupped her pert backside and lifted, revelling in the way she instinctively wrapped her legs around his hips and looped her arms around his neck, enabling him to carry her wherever it pleased him to go.

And it definitely pleased him.

It was like a roar inside him, and the longer they'd been talking, the louder it had grown. And if sleeping with her again was the only way to silence it, then he didn't care how many of his self-imposed rules he needed to break, he intended to silence it.

He had to. Because, whether it was merely physical or not, this driving need for her was beginning to cloud every other thought in his head. And that couldn't be allowed.

Unless, of course, he used it to his advantage.

As the idea began to take root, Bas found himself nurturing it. Cultivating it. If he could have her long enough, indulge in this inexplicable greed he felt when he thought of her, then surely he would be able to sate this irrational need he had for her.

And then, perhaps, he could finally get back to the life that had been just fine—more than just fine—for him, right up until a few months ago.

Crossing the room, he set her gently on the edge of his desk, his hands still holding her tightly. Still keeping her against him. Her heat against the hardest part of him, making him burn.

Lord, how he burned.

Like staring into the fiery pit of a volcano, only to then hurl himself off the rim and into the swirling orange and white depths.

He'd never felt anything like it in his life before—this need to have her that was, incomprehensibly, even more urgent than the need that had poured through him the night of the gala.

He was halfway to going mad and he didn't seem to care. Just as long as he got to taste every last millimetre of her silken skin, all over again. He didn't realise he'd murmured his intentions aloud until she moaned softly.

'We…shouldn't…'

'I told you…' He heard his voice but didn't recognise it. 'These are your consequences. Your punishment for skipping out on the lesson too early.'

'I feel appropriately disciplined,' she muttered against his mouth.

And he didn't care to examine what bolted through him at that. Instead, he trailed his hands down her sides, using his knuckles to graze the indent of her waist before allowing his fingers to spread out and his palms to cup the silken skin of her backside. And still he wanted more.

Much more. He needed to slow himself down.

'Do you know how much I like that smart mouth of yours?' he muttered, laying gentle kisses first on one corner, then the other, then back again.

Each time moving in a fraction.

'You do?' Naomi murmured softly, letting him do as he pleased.

Which, in itself, was a turn-on.

'Very much.' He repeated the action again. 'Not least when you aren't using it to take a swipe at me.'

Before she could come back with some inevitable retort, he drew back, his eyes locked with hers as he slowly, deliberately, unbuttoned the first few buttons of her tunic top, to reveal her lacy bra.

Burgundy velvet, like wine against her dark, silken skin. Flowers that cupped the bottom and adorned the top. And between the two, a sheer lace that did nothing to hide the pert, hard nipples that he now knew had haunted his dreams with their vivid, perfect detail.

He hooked one cup down to expose her.

'Bas...' she breathed on a choppy breath.

He didn't bother to answer. Instead, he simply lowered his head to capture it in his mouth, and was rewarded with a soft, raw sound from Naomi as she laced her hand through his hair and arched into him.

It was enough to make the blood pound even harder through him. Making his sex so hard that he wasn't sure how much longer he could keep taking things slowly.

But he had to. This time, this moment, was for her.

Over and over, he used his mouth, his tongue, to lavish attention on her, drawing whorls before taking her deeper into his mouth. Vaguely, he considered that she seemed even more sensitive than she had last time.

As though something was somehow...different. Though he wasn't sure that it made any sense, and he didn't care to waste time analysing it further.

Pushing it from his mind, Bas allowed his free hand to wander down her obliques, feeling her shiver as his fingers skimmed her. Then lower. Until he was sliding it under her waistband and between her legs, into the hot, wet heat that he remembered all too well.

The low, ragged sounds she made tore through him. They made him feel wild, and jagged, from the inside out. His body ached for her so badly that it was almost painful, and it cost him far more than it should have done to keep his rhythm slow. To build up a pace the way he would normally have done without even thinking twice.

It had been like this that one night, too. As if his thirst for her would never be sated. No other woman had ever made him feel quite so primitive. Obviously, it was simply a matter of chemistry, of biology, and it would wear off at some point even if it took slightly longer than usual. And even though, logically, Bas knew this, it didn't seem to help now, when he was finally alone with her again, and she was arching that magnificent body of hers against him, so wet and so hot in the palm of his hand.

Everything about Naomi had him hard and ready. As if he wanted her too much. As if he was barely in control of himself when he was around her.

And then, without warning, she grabbed his wrist and yanked it away, with a low moan as though the action had cost her far more than it cost him.

'Bas…' Her voice was strangled as she fought to pull her clothes back into place. 'I'm sorry, I can't…this can't…'

He was barely about to think over the roaring of his blood but somehow he made himself take a step back.

More than anything else, though, it was the utter shock on her face that felt like the physical slap that he surely deserved.

'This will never happen again,' he managed. 'You have my word.'

'You don't understand...' she began, but he didn't want to hear it.

Clearly, he'd misjudged the situation horribly. He, who was infamous for reading women.

'I apologise,' he bit out. 'Whole-heartedly. Unreservedly...'

'I'm pregnant.' She shook her head as if she couldn't believe what she'd just said. 'I'm sorry... this wasn't the way I wanted it to come out but... there it is.'

Bas stopped talking.

He wanted to sit down. Grab something to steady himself. Something. But, right in this moment, he couldn't see anywhere to do it. So he made himself stand straight. Maybe if he acted in control, it would make it so.

'You're pregnant?'

But he certainly didn't expect to sound so redundant.

How had he failed to notice it? To *feel* it?

Had he been that caught up in banishing the ghosts of that night that he'd failed to spot the blindingly obvious? What was it about this woman that had him acting so completely out of character?

But, of course, it wasn't about Naomi at all, was it? It was about the fact that the first time he'd met her he'd been reeling from the shock of the first damned letter.

And, right now, he was still processing the contents of the latest letter.

Of course, that was it. It made sense.

So why wasn't he as convinced as he should have been?

In front of him, Naomi was nodding slowly.

'I'm pregnant,' she confirmed, more firmly this time.

And then there was only one other question rampaging through his head.

'How far along are you, Naomi?'

CHAPTER FOUR

IT WAS THE expression on his face that thudded through Naomi the hardest—somewhere between fury and despair. It left her with the oddest impression that her confession had left him scraped hollow. Raw. Tricked.

But could she blame him—the way she'd blurted it out? What happened to any of the multitude of dignified, eloquent speeches she'd rehearsed these past months? Even now, her brain scrabbled around for words as though she were struggling to speak in some bizarre alien language.

Then again, discussing her baby with Bas certainly felt rather alien.

'It wasn't planned,' she managed, struggling to process the simple question as her heart hammered so hard in her chest that she was afraid it was going to break out any moment.

She had never shied away from difficult conversations. Whether it was delivering difficult news to a patient's family or challenging her chief of staff at the hospital, she always seemed to have just the knack for turning the conversation so that they somehow ended up thanking her for telling them the thing they hadn't wanted to hear.

'How far along are you?' he repeated, his voice barely recognisable.

No, she'd never feared awkward conversations…

but right now, if she could have avoided the one she needed to have with a certain Basilius Jansen, then she would happily have turned around and walked away.

Fled, if she was going to be honest.

Fleeing, however, wasn't exactly an option. She slowed her breathing and tried to control her racing heart.

'Twenty weeks.'

She waited a beat, her eyes not leaving Bas's face.

'Twenty weeks?' He eyed her cynically. 'You don't look twenty weeks. You don't look any weeks.'

'The tunic hides a small bump.' She shrugged as casually as she could, though it felt awkward. Wooden. 'Apparently, I'm what's called "very neat". My mother was, too. Both when she was pregnant with me, and with my sister. According to my grandmother, no one even suspected she was pregnant either time, until she was over six months gone.'

'How…convenient.'

'Not really.' Another shrug. 'It's just a fact. One study showed that one in around two and half thousand pregnant women don't know they're pregnant until they're actually in labour. Do you know that makes it three times more likely to happen than having triplets?'

'You're throwing facts around like they change anything,' he bit out, silencing her slightly manic rambling—for which she was grateful. 'The simple fact is that you're pregnant and you were prepared to let this...*thing* happen between us.'

Her heart picked up a beat.

'Why do you think I stopped you?' Her voice cracked but she pushed on. 'Why do you think I told you?'

He glowered at her harder.

'Twenty weeks ago was the week of the gala.'

'Yes.'

'You were already pregnant when you slept with me.' His low voice rumbled around her. Through her.

She could barely contain her horror.

'*No!* It happened...at the gala, of course.'

'After you were with me?' he growled, as though daring her to say otherwise.

Shock made her curt.

'Are you seriously suggesting that I slept with someone else the same night?'

He eyed her harder, but this time she refused to look away.

'All right, maybe not the same night,' he answered at last. Darkly. 'But maybe within the couple of days of the gala.'

'No.'

'You're sure?'

'I can count a calendar, thank you very much.' Her voice was much too clipped, but there was nothing she could do about that. She'd been dreading this conversation ever since she'd learned the news herself.

'I'm absolutely certain.'

Still, she couldn't drag her eyes from him as she watched something she couldn't quite identify chase across his features.

'Of course you are,' he told her thickly. 'Jansen money would tend to make a woman "absolutely certain" of the timings that would work best.'

Was he actually saying…?

'You're accusing me of getting pregnant with someone else and pinning it on you?' Indignation sent her voice higher pitched than she could have imagined.

Bas, however, remained unmoved.

'Are you?'

Her stomach tilted and churned.

'I understand that the Jansen name is a draw…' She fought to bring her voice back down to something resembling normal. 'But that would be pretty desperate.'

It was an appeal to his sense of decency, but the expression on his face didn't change. If anything, the one thing that flitted across it was so bleak that it made her breath catch.

'People can be desperate. Sometimes, their lies work—for a time. But when the truth comes out, the baby is the one who ultimately pays the price.'

She didn't know how to answer, and so she didn't. And as the clock on the wall ticked the time away, the silence pressed in on her—close, and stifling. She found herself licking her lips, hating herself for the moment of weakness.

'I'm not lying.'

'No.' His voice was dangerously even. 'Because, as you said, you're "absolutely certain".'

Naomi drew in another breath as decades of self-preservation kicked in. She lifted her head and forced herself to meet his eye. She would not cower. She would not make apologies.

'Because you're the only person I've slept with in a year.'

Bas's eyes bored into her for what felt like an age.

'Repeat that,' he demanded, at last.

At least he sounded as unbalanced as she felt. Still, it had taken all she had to say it once, so how was she supposed to say it again?

'I'm the only person you've slept with?' he answered for her, when she didn't speak.

'In a year,' she managed quietly. 'Yes.'

She'd had a couple of boyfriends in the past, so he wasn't the only man with whom she'd ever had a sexual relationship.

But he was the only one who had shown her that it could be that intense, incredible thing that she'd only ever seen in the movies Leila loved to watch. And still, he couldn't have looked any more winded if she'd landed a sucker punch right in his gut.

To his credit, he recovered swiftly.

Of course he did—because Basilius Jansen

wasn't just the King of Smooth, he was the damned Emperor of it. Notorious for both his charm and his smooth tongue.

Though perhaps best not to think about the latter too closely. Naomi suppressed a thrilling shiver of awareness.

'Okay.' He folded his arms over his chest, which did little to alleviate the churning ocean that was rushing inside her. 'So you're claiming that this baby is mine?'

'I'm not *claiming*. I'm stating. It's a fact.' This was even harder than she'd anticipated. 'Run a paternity test if you like—the non-invasive prenatal paternity can be done after eight weeks. In case you still doubt me, let me remind you that I'm twenty weeks along.'

It was the nightmare that she'd feared facing yet, at the same time, at least she was finally telling him. Fifteen weeks for her to get used to the idea herself. And fifteen weeks of batting back and forth in her mind: did she tell him, or didn't she? Naomi felt an overwhelming sense of relief that she was finally doing what she believed was the right thing. Whatever the outcome.

She couldn't back out now.

'Insisting isn't going to make me suddenly believe.'

'Then do the damned test, Bas,' she cried, her impatience running out without warning.

And if her voice sounded thicker than usual, then

she was probably the only one of the two of them who knew it.

'They'll take a sample of my blood containing foetal DNA, and yours, then employ parallel sequencing and analysing over two and a half thousand genetic markers. It's about as accurate as you can get—ninety-nine point nine-nine per cent, if you want the figures.'

'I know what NIPP is, Naomi,' he bit out oddly. As though he were speaking to her from much further away than the other side of the room.

An inappropriate gurgle of amusement made its way up her chest. Nerves. Not that knowing that helped her in that moment. Bas looked as though he were the one who had just been hit by a car, rather than her.

And not just a car—more like a ruddy great freight train.

'What is it that you hope to gain from this?' he demanded abruptly, making her feel rooted to the pristine floor.

Vulnerable.

She hated that part the most.

'I don't hope to gain anything from you.' The words tumbled out. '*We* don't hope to gain anything.'

'Then you've decided to keep it.'

'I have,' she confirmed. 'I know there are other choices, especially for a single mum who is supposed to be retraining to become a doctor. I know the hours would have been long enough without a baby to have to juggle, too. I could have terminated. Or I could put him up for adoption. But… this is my choice.'

Even if it hadn't been part of any plan.

In truth, up until she'd been sitting in her cramped bathroom, in the flat she'd bought for herself, and her grandmother, and her kid sister, Naomi hadn't even been sure she'd ever wanted children.

She knew how to raise a kid, sure—she'd been more of a mother to her sister than a sibling. But then, she'd had to be. Her own mother wasn't much of an example, and her grandmother was too soft. And too busy working two jobs, even into her sixties.

From the moment she'd found out she was pregnant, she'd flip-flopped from one option to another, to another, then back again. Until now she was here, twenty weeks in and finally telling her baby's father the news.

Apparently, she'd made her decision.

'And you're telling me about it out of the goodness of your heart?' Bas demanded curtly.

Warily, she thought.

Naomi shook her head.

'I'm telling you because it's the right thing to do.'

'But you don't want anything.

It wasn't a question. It was a cynical statement. One that told her that Bas didn't believe a word she was saying.

'Not a thing. I can take care of myself.' Then, before she could stop herself, 'I've been doing it for long enough.'

There was a flash of something in his eyes at that, and she could have kicked herself for the slip-up. Since when did she share with anyone about her private life?

'That's as may be.' He glowered at her. 'But I'm willing to bet you aren't used to taking care of yourself whilst pregnant.'

Naomi took another breath.

'So you believe it's your baby.'

He cast her a sceptical look.

'I believe you're pregnant,' Bas clarified. 'Whether or not it's my baby remains to be seen.'

She swallowed back a snarky response.

'It's yours. There was no one else.'

'So you keep saying.'

'Fine. Then I won't say it any more. The fact is that I told you. I knew you wouldn't be interested but I told you anyway. There. That's it. I've done my moral duty.'

She wasn't sure how, but somehow Naomi managed to turn around and make her way to the door. But as she reached for the handle his voice cracked through the air like thunder, though he barely even raised it.

'Don't even think about opening that door.'

She froze as the air tightened in the room.

Slowly, slowly, she turned.

'I can't imagine there's anything more you could possibly say,' she choked out. 'Nothing civil, at any rate.'

'Believe me, I haven't yet even started with what I have to say.'

She twisted her arm and cast a pointed glance at her watch.

'Then you'd better hurry up. There's another gala tonight. And maybe another lucky woman waiting for you to knock her up.'

She didn't need the steel in the air to know that she'd gone too far. But the whole situation was so stressful, was it really any surprise the moment had got to her?

'I'm sorry… I didn't mean…'

Bas didn't answer. Instead he watched her a moment longer, then pulled his mobile out of his pocket and punched in a couple of keys.

'Who are you calling?' She frowned, craning her neck and hating herself for not biting her question back.

He put the phone to his ear and cast her a black look.

'When was the last time you had a scan?'

'A scan?' Naomi frowned at him. 'About a month ago. Why?'

'I'd like to see it.'

She heard the phone ring, and then the sound of a robotic answerphone voice as Bas rang off irritably.

'By "it" I presume you mean the baby. Why?'

She eyed him suspiciously. 'Because you think I'm lying?'

'You know what they say about a picture painting a thousand words,' he clipped out instead.

Her glower was nothing short of murderous, but he seemed frustratingly immune to it.

'I offered to take a paternity test,' she pointed out.

'I find I wish to see a scan.'

'No.'

'*No?*' he repeated slowly, his head snapping up.

It seemed the short refusal had caught him off-guard, but Naomi refused to feel guilty.

'A paternity test can be carried out relatively anonymously. It can be sent away to people who don't know either of us. But if you came to a scan with me, people would see us.

'Do you really think you'll be able to keep your pregnancy a secret indefinitely? Perhaps I should explain a few things about the pregnancy process.'

'Don't be so condescending.' Naomi sniffed at him.

He cast her a strange look and she got the impression that no one ever sniffed at him. She doubted anyone dared.

'People *will* find out, Naomi. Eventually.'

'I know people are going to find out eventually,' she pressed on. 'And I'll be talked about as the new trainee doctor who fell pregnant her first month here. But I don't need to be the new trainee doctor who fell pregnant her first week here, and the father is Thorncroft's very own Lothario Basilius Jansen.'

'Except that's exactly the scenario,' he commented cheerily. 'Might as well face up to it now.'

'No,' she ground out again. 'Though perhaps I should be grateful you're no longer accusing me of sleeping with anyone else the same night I was with you.'

'Don't push it, Naomi,' Bas growled. 'At this point, I'm not ruling anything out.

'So you'd rather no one here knew you were pregnant? Or just that there's no father?'

'I'd rather people minded their own business,' she corrected. 'But, in the event that I choose to explain further, I'll just tell them that he's someone from before I moved back here.'

Anything but admit it was him, clearly. A sharp expression clouded Bas's face and Naomi tried to look marginally apologetic.

'The point is, it would cause too much of a stir if you attended a scan with me. Practically the whole hospital would know about it, and for what? It isn't as though you're going to even be a part of its life.'

'You have to tell people at some point,' he pointed out, scathingly. 'What about Thorncroft as your employer? Or us, as the benefactors of your Jansen Bursary? I'm certain there's a legal obligation.'

'Not precisely, since I had no intention of taking time off work, even for maternity leave.' Not so much through choice, more through necessity, though he didn't need to know that. 'But if I *had* wanted statutory maternity leave then I'd have to inform the hospital by the fifteenth week before my due date. That means around week twenty-five. I still have a month to decide what I'm going to do.'

'You're not putting my child—*my* child—up for adoption. He or she will not grow up feeling as though they weren't wanted.'

She blinked. He couldn't possibly have known just how close to the knuckle that felt.

He wasn't the one who had grown up feeling as if they weren't good enough. Not dainty enough, or pretty enough. Not *enough*. He couldn't know what it felt like to be second-best. Second choice. However hard her grandmother had worked to try to ensure neither her nor Leila felt that way.

Naomi squared her shoulders, pushing past the familiar stabbing feeling.

'I thought you hadn't yet accepted that you're the father?'

To her shock, Bas stopped moving. As if he himself hadn't realised what he'd said.

'Let's just say that I've yet to be convinced,' he ground out, regrouping at last. 'But if that baby is indeed mine, then you won't be discarding them like the bins you put out on rubbish day.'

The ferocity in his words caught Naomi off guard. And she didn't know what it was about them, but they riled her instantly.

'I would never *discard* my baby,' she hissed. 'I'm talking about putting my child's needs ahead of my own. We can't all be the son of some famous surgeon, living some charmed life.'

'I'd advise you to stop there, Naomi,' Bas warned.

And any other time she might have heeded the strange note to his voice. But she was too full of indignation.

'My mother kept me and my sister—half-sister, if we're going to be pedantic—but she wasn't in a position to look after either of us. She certainly couldn't love us. But she insisted on keeping us. Right up until she couldn't cope any longer and my grandmother had to take over. And, as much as my grandmother provided for us, and loved us, she was old, and tired, and she wasn't our mother. And didn't every other kid in school remind us of that fact?'

'At least you had someone who wanted to do what was morally right and be there for you,' Bas replied, his stilted voice gouging at her. 'And at least, as you said, she loved you.'

'What's that supposed to mean?'

But whatever he'd been thinking, he'd shut it down now, and he shook his head. Punching the keys on his phone again, he turned to her, his voice even but inflexible.

'I want to see a scan, Naomi. And I intend for you to get one. But, for what it's worth, we'll be discreet.

'There's no such thing as discreet in this place,' she scorned. 'I don't want the whole hospital gossiping about me. Worse, someone might remember seeing us leave the gala around the same time and put two and two together.'

He eyed her sharply.

'Plenty of women would revel in being pregnant with my baby. They wouldn't hesitate in letting the entire hospital know.'

'I'm not "plenty of women",' she harrumphed.

'No,' he stated—somewhat cryptically in Naomi's opinion. 'You are not.'

She practically had to bite her tongue not to ask him exactly what he mean by that. It didn't matter much anyway. He was already talking to someone on his mobile.

'Grace? Call me back as soon as you get this. It's urgent.'

Not *someone*, then. But that robotic answerphone voice. Still, for a notoriously single man, Naomi couldn't help but wonder who the woman was.

Not that she was jealous, of course, she reminded herself hastily. She and Bas had enjoyed a one-night stand—not even that long. No strings, and all that. She knew the drill—even if she wasn't exactly practised in it.

Who was she kidding? She'd never had one before—not even once—it was something Leila had scorned her for many times. *Prim, uptight Naomi.*

And now look at her. Pregnant the first time she'd tried to cut loose. She was a walking cliché, so the last thing she intended to do was compound it by acting like some jealous stalker.

She tried to sound casual. Or neutral, at the very least.

'Who's Grace?'

He eyed her, almost disparagingly.

'A friend.'

Naomi wrinkled her nose.

'That's hardly helpful,' she pointed out. 'Or do you make a habit of placing random calls when women tell you they're pregnant?'

'Women don't customarily tell me they're pregnant.'

He lifted his shoulders in what could be considered to be a shrug, but was so overtly masculine it made her body clench tightly.

'At least, a few have tried it but they've disappeared satisfyingly quickly when asked to provide evidence of their claim. Especially since I am always very careful to take…precautions.'

Naomi suppressed a delicious shiver.

Yes, she remembered his precautions. She'd even tried to roll it on for him. She could only presume that, in her haste and inexperience, she'd snagged it with the stick-on nails that her sister had insisted on her wearing for the ball.

Not long, or gaudy—quite pretty, actually—but not ideal for sliding on bits of delicate rubber.

And she really needed to stop picturing the image, or she was going to heat up so much that she might set the hospital sprinkler system off. And then she might have a different problem, because the image of Bas in a wet suit as it clung to his muscles was a whole other minefield.

She licked her lips.

'Is that your way of saying you want a paternity test?'

This was the moment she'd been expecting. Waiting for. In many ways, she was almost shocked he hadn't ejected her from the entire wing at the first mention of pregnancy. Just so that she wouldn't sully his reputable name any further.

Yet, Bas stared at her, taking far too long to answer her.

'That will come, of course,' he managed eventually, and she had the oddest impression that it hadn't actually even crossed his mind.

But that couldn't be right, either.

'First, however, we're going for a scan.'

Fear rose in Naomi's chest.

'We most certainly are not. I told you, I don't want the entire hospital gossiping about me, which will be inevitable if they know I'm pregnant. Let alone if you're the one accompanying me. I've had a scan. Everything was fine. I am definitely *not* going for another with you.'

He cast her a cool look.

'Are you quite finished with your rant?'

'I'm not being *that* conversion nurse who got pregnant with Bas Jensen's baby.'

'And you won't be. Grace is utterly discreet and she will come here.'

'No.' Naomi shook her head.

'You will have that scan, Naomi. And I will be with you.' He folded his arms again, and this time she was struck by quite how authoritative the man was. How had she failed to appreciate quite what *power* looked like on a man? He didn't just bear the Jensen name, rather he epitomised everything it represented.

She glowered at him, but it seemed to bounce off his solid chest without making a dent.

'So you're…what? Taking charge now?' The idea of it should baulk more. So why didn't it? 'I told you, I don't need your help, I'm perfectly used to taking care of myself.'

'And I'm beginning to think you *tell* me a few too many things whilst you aren't as keen to listen. But I suspect that part of the reason for telling me now is because this is beginning to overwhelm you.'

'You're deluded.'

'No, I'm not, but I think you are.' His voice dropped to a sudden, quiet hum. 'I suspect that whether you want to admit it or not, deep down, you don't want to be the one taking care of everything. You want someone to take the reins for once.'

And it was odd, but it was still there, that lethal air, swirling beneath the surface like a rip tide, just waiting to drag her under. But he was controlling it with a fierceness that struck an unexpected chord in her.

As though by controlling that, he could control some dark secret of his own. As if a man like him had dark secrets at all.

Naomi laughed. Less humour, more a slightly maniacal sound.

She didn't intend to, it just bubbled up out of nowhere, taking over her until her shoulders were shaking and her arms were around her chest. And if there was a slightly maniacal edge to it, then surely she was the only one who could tell?

Because it struck her that she really was out of her depth with this pregnancy. And perhaps his assessment of her wasn't so ludicrous, after all.

So where did that leave her?

'I'm taking you home,' Bas announced abruptly. 'We'll arrange the scan for tomorrow.'

She fought to sober up.

'I'm still on duty.'

'You're done.'

'I don't think so.' She shook her head as he indicated the wall clock behind her.

'Your shift should have finished over an hour ago.'

She shouldn't feel flattered that he'd paid that much attention earlier. He clearly didn't intend it as such.

'Fine, but I don't need a lift. I'm perfectly capable of making my own way home.'

'Do you have your car back?'

His eyes held hers steadily.

'My car?' She wrinkled her nose.

He couldn't possibly have remembered.

'I seem to recall you mentioning that your sister had your car these days. For college, I believe.'

She'd told him that the night of the gala. She hadn't known why. A random conversation they'd been having on the lead up to them being intimate. The fact that he remembered all this time later was…surprising. And Naomi refused to read anything more into it than that.

'My sister still has my car,' she admitted. 'But there are buses running every half-hour from the main stop outside the hospital.'

'And you'd rather wait in the cold night, then endure a long stop-start journey home, than accept a lift from me?'

She would, as it happened. Because whether she wanted to admit it or not, she would rather he didn't see where she lived. Not that she wasn't proud of the fact that she'd bought the two-bed flat for her family, it was just that when she compared it to the luxury penthouse she imagined Bas owned, she felt a little…lacking.

'I'm perfectly…'

'Capable of looking after yourself. Yes, so you've said.' He sounded distinctly unconcerned. 'However, that was before you were carrying this baby—*my* baby.'

'I don't need clarification,' she reminded him. 'I'm not the one who has been in any doubt about its parentage.'

He chose not to answer that.

'You will not be getting the bus any more.'

A smile tugged at the corners of her mouth, despite the prickling indignation.

'You say the word "bus" as though it appals you.'

'Are you suggesting you enjoy such a journey?'

'Sure.' Naomi nodded. 'It gives me time to think. An hour where I can quietly process whatever happened in work that day. Anyway, it's called the real world. You ought to try it one day instead of all your supercars and private jets.'

'I think not.'

She stifled a giggle. If he'd been appalled before, he sounded positively horrified now. And she couldn't explain why needling him was such fun. She made herself shrug.

'Shame. You might find the real world isn't anywhere near as bad as you think.'

She might have known he wouldn't let her have the upper hand for long.

'Are you scared of me, Naomi? Do you think I'll bite?'

It took everything she had not to startle at that. Just, she suspected, as he'd intended. And now her entire body was once again prickling with awareness, and with the too-vivid recollections of their night—hours—together. As though she wanted a repeat performance.

Worse, as though she wanted more—when of course she didn't. And the disdainful man in front of her clearly didn't, either.

Yet still, she found herself following him out of his office, and down the quiet, sleek Jansen wing corridors, and to the exclusive car park reserved for the private wing's consultants only.

Without exception, the cars were all new, high-end motors. Even so, Naomi wasn't remotely surprised when Bas led her to the most muscular, uncompromisingly styled supercar of the lot.

Totally impractical for a baby, of course, she couldn't help thinking. As if that would ever be a factor for the great Bas.

'Of course not.' She forced herself to laugh, but it sounded far more brittle than she would have preferred.

'Because you know I won't,' Bas continued, far too breezily.

'I know,' she managed.

'Not even for you, *älskling.*' His grin was utterly wicked yet icily cold. 'After what you've done, not even if you ask really nicely.'

CHAPTER FIVE

BAS GRIPPED THE steering wheel tighter as he skilfully manoeuvred through the parking garage, and out onto the main road, and tried to focus on his driving. Anything that kept that tumult in his head at bay.

Now that the initial shock was beginning to recede, he could feel a fury beginning to stir. Naomi was twenty weeks pregnant, and he was only just finding out about it now.

If he hadn't walked into that resus bay, today, with her patient, if he hadn't bumped into her— would she even be telling him now?

The question threw itself angrily around his head. He needed answers, but not now. Not until he knew he could keep his cool.

'Left or right at the junction?' he demanded coldly, instead.

'Left or right?' Naomi echoed uncertainly, and a less than forgiving side of himself felt a grim satisfaction at the tremor in her voice. The one he knew she'd hoped she'd concealed from him. It betrayed how much she was struggling right now.

Good—she deserved to.

'Where do you live, Naomi?'

'Oh…' She drew in a sharp breath, before giving him her address.

He didn't know the area well—certainly not

somewhere he'd visited—but he knew the direction. Slipping expertly through the gears, Bas nosed his car in the appropriate direction. It would be quicker to drop onto the motorway, maybe about a twenty-minute journey, but public transport would surely have to take at least three or four times that—and only if she didn't have to change buses.

Not that Naomi's transport arrangements were his concern, he reminded himself hastily. Or his problem.

Aside from the one, obvious fact that she was pregnant with his child. *Allegedly his child,* he reminded himself again.

He had never intended to become a father. Never intended to settle down. He knew only too well that he wasn't capable of the kind of selfless love that set a good husband, and good father apart from a bad one.

He was a potent combination of the worst traits of both his parents, and probably those violent step-fathers, too—and there was no damned way he was going to pass that on to anyone else. He would never inflict his childhood on any other poor, innocent kid.

It was why he'd planned his life's trajectory down to the finest detail. Why he'd always been so fastidious about protection. And yet, ever since that kiss with her had brought the memories of that night with Naomi crashing back—he could now remember events in all too glorious detail.

He could picture exactly how she'd looked when she'd watched him take the condom from his jacket pocket, her eyes so dark, and innocent, and greedy, her breathing catching in throat with every shallow, choppy intake, that he'd feared he might have embarrassed himself on the spot.

The way she'd taken it from him had been captivating, her hands actually shaking with the same need that had been tearing through him, right in that moment. Her obvious inexperience had been ridiculously captivating, resulting in him feeling like some unschooled adolescent rather than the notorious playboy of Thorncroft.

Little wonder, then, that the condom had failed and he now found himself in the situation he'd spent his entire adult life avoiding.

Naomi was pregnant.

The knowledge kept clattering around Bas's head, which felt altogether too empty. Too echoing. He felt suffocated, as though the very breath were being squeezed from his lungs. Yes, Naomi was pregnant, and he was going to be a father.

Him—who should be the last person on Earth to ever subject a child to him as a parent.

Something sharp lodged within Bas's chest. He ignored it.

She was right about the fact that he ought to be demanding paternity tests. His first phone call should have been to his lawyers. They had a series of protocols in place for just such an event—his father had ensured that, being an even more infamous playboy surgeon than his son.

In fact, the protocols had been set up the very week that Magnus had discovered he had a seven-year-old son—two seven-year-old sons, in fact—and that one of them was being foisted upon him.

'Come off at the junction coming up.' Naomi's tight voice broke into his thoughts. 'Then take the second exit. It'll drop you straight onto some country lanes.'

He grunted his acknowledgement, flicking the signal to switch lanes, but didn't add anything more.

Thinking about his twin brother—and the letter still lying in his office bin—didn't help. As ridiculous a notion as it was, he'd felt as if the damned unread letter were judging him. In all the ruckus, he'd forgotten that Henrik had declared his intention to attend tonight's gala. He'd been preparing all day to do damage control, but, after Naomi's revelation, attending the ball was the furthest thing from Bas's mind.

Another thing to ask Grace to take on for him, when she finally got around to returning his damned answerphone message.

As he pulled off the motorway and onto the country lanes that Naomi had indicated, an odd feeling moved through Bas.

The road twisted and turned whilst the built-up environs of the city gave way to flatter, green areas and, as his car began to roar through the relatively traffic-free lanes, for a brief moment Bas began to feel a little less suffocated.

For five or ten minutes, as the car clung masterfully to the tight bends and accelerated through the straights, Bas felt free. But he might have known it wouldn't last. A couple more turns and the road began with ribbon housing and then, suddenly, they were in another built-up area. With an older high street and tired buildings.

The reality of the situation crashed back in.

Bas knew what his father would tell—or, more accurately, *command*—him to do once the indomitable Magnus Jansen heard the news about Naomi. Namely to agree a generous monthly sum to be paid from the lawyers directly into her account. An amount that would be more than enough to take care of this unborn child, as well as to ensure that Naomi signed a non-disclosure form to prevent her from ever telling anyone that he was father to a child. And get back to living his life exactly as before.

It was known as the Erin Contract, and it was what Magnus had put in place straight after he'd been burned by the woman who Bas barely remembered but who was, for all intents and purposes, his biological mother.

She was also the woman who had thrown him away without a second thought when Henrik had thrown him to the wolves.

And didn't that tell him everything he'd already known his entire life? Didn't that prove just how disposable he was? How, as a kid, both his mother and his twin brother had found him that easy to discard.

Magnus had been the one to catch him—though his father had never hidden the fact that it was out of a sense of obligation rather than love. Even growing up, nothing he'd done had been good enough for them. Only Mrs Jenkins, the housekeeper and cook at Redlington Castle—the country pile Magnus had purchased but rarely visited, and where Bas had grown up—had ever shown him love.

It had only been when he'd shown an aptitude for medicine that his father had finally taken notice. And more because the man had realised his son becoming a successful surgeon could reflect well on himself and the Jansen name.

Even so, whilst living with Magnus Jansen might have afforded him a luxury lifestyle, he'd still had to work bloody hard to become the surgeon he was today. Not least because Magnus hadn't so much opened doors for him as shoved his foot behind them to stop Bas from coming through.

The last thing the old man had wanted was to be eclipsed by a kid. Even his own. And even for himself, no amount of success could ever entirely erase the feeling of spending the first two and a half decades of his life hatefully unwanted. Discarded first by his mother, in part down to Henrik, and then resented by his father.

So why would he choose to inflict that kind of upbringing on any child of his own? All those hard, spiteful lessons? And he would inflict them—it wasn't as though he knew any other way to do it.

This was precisely why Magnus had contingency plans with lawyers. He could walk away from Naomi whilst ensuring that his child was more than generously compensated. It would have a better life than Naomi could ever provide herself—on the single proviso that she never publicly named him as the father.

The proverbial win-win. All he had to do was pick up the phone and call his lawyers.

So why wasn't he doing just that?

Why wasn't he kicking Naomi out of the door, and refusing to have any conversation with her until he even knew for sure that the child she claimed was his *was*, in fact, his?

He could blame it on this unexpected, wholly inappropriate, and entirely unwanted residual attraction, of course. The unwelcome fact that he still wanted her. Had wanted her ever since that night when he'd waited for her in that shower, only to discover that she'd snuck out of the hotel room.

He should have revelled in it. No pouting and no preening as she'd tried to convince him that their brief intimacy was actually the start of something new and wonderful together. No tears and no tantrums when he would have stood up, dressed, and assured her that this would never happen again.

Instead, his bed that night had simply felt cold. Empty. Without her in it. And he hadn't wanted any other woman to fill it, ever since.

Bas thought it was that truth that galled him the most. Even now, he couldn't pinpoint what it was about her that affected him so very deeply. As no one else ever had.

Presumably that was why he hadn't been acting with his head from the moment she'd dropped her bombshell on him. The reason why, despite his arguments to the contrary, a part of him had believed it was his baby the moment she'd told him it was. And the reason why he was driving out of his way into a less salubrious area of the city, just to ensure that the mother of his child was safe.

And he hated himself for such weakness.

Well, no more. As soon as he dropped her at home, he was heading back to the city, back to civilisation, and back to the lawyers who could handle the rest of this unpleasant debacle without him having to sully his hands any further. Something about this thought made Bas feel even more unsettled than he had since Naomi had appeared back in his life. But he wouldn't think about that now. He had years of practice pushing uncomfortable thoughts to hidden recesses of his brain. And what was one more to add to his already existing multitude of unpleasant memories...?

* * *

'Take a left, then the second right.'

Her quiet voice cut through his thoughts.

He peered through the top of the windscreen and grimaced.

'These are flats.'

'So they are,' she agreed, valiantly attempting to convince herself that she didn't give a rat's backside what he thought about her. 'Mine's the one on the right, next to the field.'

'Here?' He made no effort to conceal his distaste. 'This is where you live?'

'We don't all have the Jansen name. Or money.'

Could he practically feel her bristling in her seat? She probably ought to be more circumspect; he'd been remarkably patient, not levelling half the demands or accusations at her that she'd tried to anticipate he might.

But her usual patient, judicious self appeared to have deserted her. What was it about this man that left her feeling so edgy, so impatient, so unlike herself?

'Still, you're a doctor, you must have some money. This place is barely a step up from student digs.'

'Hardly.' Naomi snorted, refusing to acknowledge the heat blooming in her cheeks, and spreading down her neck even as she scrabbled for the button to raise the door. 'It's actually quite decent. Though I can imagine anything less than millionaire penthouses look like hovels to you.'

'Hardly.'

'You have no right to try to shame me.' She threw the door open before he could get around to open it for her. 'You were born with a proverbial silver spoon in your mouth. A monied plastic surgeon for a father, opening doors for you by virtue of the Jansen name alone. And that's fine, but don't judge the rest of us mere mortals.'

But just because she had got the door open didn't mean she'd managed to unfold herself out before he was there, holding his hand out to her as though she were some kind of old woman.

Or pregnant.

'What are you doing?' Naomi gritted her teeth and glared up at him from the passenger seat.

'Do I need to worry about my car around here whilst I walk you to the door?' he asked, his tone deliberately neutral as he ignored her question.

Her jaw locked tighter, if that were possible.

'We're not complete heathens around here. Not that it matters anyway. I can walk twenty metres on my own.'

'Is that so?' he pondered, almost cheerfully. 'Then I won't be walking with you for long.'

'No,' she snapped.

'Yes. Now, I don't mind if you want to stand on the street and cause a scene, but if you really don't want to be on the hospital grapevine by tomorrow, as you've declared several times already, then I suggest you tell me where we're heading. Before someone sees us.'

Naomi lurched angrily out of the car, and across the pavement to her crumbling, old building, wishing she weren't picturing it through his eyes. He'd never had to claw for every little thing the way she had. Taking care of a baby sister and grandmother whilst trying to scrape the money together to fund the years studying for the career she'd always wanted.

She'd been so proud of being able to buy this little place a few years earlier. Yes, she had the mortgage to pay but it had meant, for the first time, that they hadn't been reliant on a landlord. There was no one putting up the rent, no spending time and love trying to make it nice, only for some less than scrupulous landlord to turf them out.

Yanking open the door, she dimly realised he was taking the weight of it from her.

'Where do you think you're going?' She wished her voice didn't hold such a note of panic.

'I'm seeing exactly where you think you're going to raise my child.'

'No.'

This time it was less a note, and more a shriek, of panic.

'The fact that you don't want me to even see your apartment tells me all I need to know,' he commented pointedly.

'It isn't that.' Naomi shook her head, but whatever else she might have wanted to say didn't come. Turning around to face Bas, she deliberately blocked the doorway. 'You can't come up.'

'The hell I can't,' he rebutted, though there was no heat to his tone.

Nothing to make her feel intimidated.

Merely…uncomfortable. Her life was so far removed from his. Had it been too much to wish that the only image he'd ever had of her was as that polished woman at the gala, who had looked as though she'd fitted into his world? If only for that one night.

'You can't come up,' she repeated. 'It isn't…that is, I don't live alone.'

She wasn't ready for the thunderous expression that darkened over his too-beautiful face.

'Say again?'

'I just mean…' She stopped, and exhaled slowly. Thoroughly. There was nothing else for it but to tell the truth and trust in his discretion not to share her private business with the entire hospital. 'I live with my grandmother and my sister.'

'Your grandmother?'

He'd managed his trick of pinning her with his gaze again, Naomi realised. And even though she knew it was irrational, it left her with an inexplicable compunction to fill the dead air.

'And my sister, yes.' She licked her lips.

'You already told me about them. The sister who has your car and the grandmother who raised you.

Granted, you didn't mention that you still lived together.'

'Right.' She hesitated, not sure why it was suddenly so important to explain how much they meant to her. 'It feels like it's always been the three of us, even before my mother died.'

Also, no need for Bas to know how.

'You never knew your father?'

'No. My grandmother took care of us, and now I try to take care of her.'

And still she stood in Bas's way, blocking the door. He could have pushed past her, of course. She wondered why he didn't. Why he chose instead to lean against the wall and simply...talk. As if he knew she needed a moment to get her head around the fact that he was here.

'And your sister's at the college just out of town, right? She must be about nineteen? What is she studying?'

'She's seventeen, and she's studying fashion. All she's ever wanted to be is a designer.' Despite the circumstances, Naomi couldn't help smiling. 'She's really good. She designed and made that emerald gown for me, for the gala.'

'She made that?'

The sudden heat in his eyes caught Naomi unawares. He stifled it in an instant, but it was too late. She'd seen it and it had already seared through her, leaving her struggling to even remember what they'd been saying.

'I bought the dress itself in a…*shop*.' She couldn't bring herself to tell him it had been a charity shop. 'It didn't look great, but I liked the material. Leila was the one who redesigned it and gave it a modern edge.'

'It was bloody stunning,' he announced gruffly, doing things to her.

'My point is…' Her chest was still fluttering wildly and it took all she had not to press her hand to it just to try to slow the beats. 'My point is that you can't come in. It isn't just my home, it's theirs, too. And…they don't know about you.'

'They don't know you're pregnant?' He eyed her sceptically.

'Obviously they know I'm pregnant. But they don't know you're the father and I have no intention of telling them.' She refused to feel guilty. 'My grandmother has gone through enough between taking on me, then Leila, and then losing my mother—her daughter. She doesn't need to know that I fell pregnant to a man who is technically my boss's son, in a hotel-room fumble after the first gala ball I ever attended in my new job.'

'So what do they think?' he demanded incredulously. 'That I'm some boyfriend who left you high and dry when I heard the news?'

'Not exactly.'

'Then what? *Exactly?*'

She bit her lip, wishing he weren't pushing her so hard.

'I told them that the father is a former colleague from my army days. But that he has been deployed.'

'You told them that?'

She pressed her lips together in a thin line, wishing she didn't have to say anything more.

'I also told them that we're going to get married when he gets back home.'

Bas stared at her incredulously, and it was as though she were actually shrinking. Pressed down by the weight of his glare.

'What then? You were going to claim he'd been killed in action?'

'No!' she cried instinctively, then paused.

What *had* she thought she was going to say? She couldn't have pretended that he was deployed for the rest of her baby's life. Shame translated itself to anger.

'You're in no position to judge. You're the king of one-night stands at Thorncroft. I was hardly going to admit to having a brief fling with the surgeon playboy, was I? I had no husband and nowhere to go. It might not hold such shock value in today's day and age, but it would with my old-fashioned grandmother.'

Naomi drew in a deep breath, preparing herself for the next onslaught. But it didn't quite come.

She'd never been so grateful for the ring of a mobile phone, and she tried not to care that Bas had practically dropped her in order to pick it up on the first ring.

'You got my message,' Bas stated, without preamble.

So this was Grace, presumably.

'I need a favour.'

Naomi strained, trying to hear the reply on the other end without appearing to Bas as though she was eavesdropping.

'Can you make it quick? I've got a consult waiting.'

'I need you to make me an appointment.'

'Really?' Naomi heard the other woman scoff. 'You aren't pregnant, Bas.'

There was silence as the woman seemed to be waiting for Bas to laugh, but he didn't. Of course he didn't. Naomi could virtually see the proverbial penny dropping.

'No? You got someone...?'

'Not *someone*,' Bas gritted out, and Naomi hated herself for the way her heart jumped.

'How far along?' the bodiless Grace asked, her voice dropping so that Naomi found herself leaning closer before she could stop herself.

'Twenty weeks.' Bas eyed her movement towards him, narrowed his glare. But at least he didn't turn away. This conversation concerned her just as much as him. He turned his attention back to Grace. 'But she isn't showing much at all. This is all done discreetly, understand? You don't mention it to anyone.'

'She might have got away with it this far, but she

won't be able to hide it for ever, Bas.' Naomi heard the woman tut softly. 'Not even much longer.'

'Thank you, I am aware. Perhaps you can tell her that yourself, however.'

'Not a chance,' Naomi heard, then tried not to bristle again when Grace added, 'This is your mess, not mine.'

'Are you going to help, or just pass judgement?' Bas snapped.

'I thought a little of both,' Grace answered airily, and Naomi found herself grudgingly liking the woman. The way she handled Bas was so simple, yet so effective. It almost made her jealous.

But, of course, that would have been nonsensical.

'How about I see you both first thing tomorrow morning? It was my day off, after the ball, but, hey, I've learned to expect the unexpected around you.'

'Dammit, the ball,' Bas gritted out, apparently belatedly remembering. 'You'll need to do something else for me. You'll have to go on my behalf and—'

He stopped abruptly, turning to look at Naomi. A shuttered expression coming down over his face. Clearly, he didn't want her to overhear whatever it was he had to say.

He turned his back.

'I just need you to look out for anything... unusual.'

Naomi couldn't hear Grace's reply, but it was

clear that the other woman hadn't understood any more than she had.

'I mean, listen out for anyone who you think… shouldn't be there. I've alerted security that they need to be ready.'

Again, the woman said something, but Naomi didn't catch it.

'I trust that you'll know it if you see it,' Bas gritted out. 'As for the scan, how about now? We can use the facilities in the Jansen wing—with the gala tonight no one should really see us there.'

Naomi waited as they agreed a time, without her. As though she—the person who was actually present—was second to the plans. So what did it say that she was letting them? Allowing them to sort it all out.

It was only when Bas had moved the phone away from his face, about to ring off, that Naomi heard Grace speak again.

'Bas, one last thing. Whatever you're thinking right now—don't.'

Bas growled in warning, but it didn't stop the woman.

'I've never thought you would be the bad father you think you would.'

'I don't wish to discuss this, Grace…'

Grace, it appeared, wasn't about to be silenced so easily. He moved his finger to terminate the call, but not before Naomi heard the other woman say one more thing.

'You're not him. And you sure as hell aren't her—'

The voice went dead as Bas swiped viciously at the screen, and then eyeballed it, unmoving.

Behind her, Naomi could hear the wind in the sycamore trees as it began to pick up. She desperately wanted to ask what Grace had meant by her comments, but something stopped her.

The moments ticked by and then, with a furious glare, Bas swung around to her.

'You have five minutes to throw what you need into a bag and meet me in the car.'

CHAPTER SIX

'I DON'T UNDERSTAND.' Naomi felt as though her entire body was shaking uncontrollably. Her heart hurtling around her chest so violently that she feared it might punch its way through altogether. 'There was nothing wrong with my baby at the last scan.'

She felt her hand being enveloped in a larger one, which she dimly realised was Bas's, but she could hardly process it. She was caught in a nightmare. This had to be her punishment for even considering the option of giving her baby up.

Or perhaps for failing to tell Bas straight away.

So this was her punishment. It was too much to bear.

'This is my fault,' she whispered.

'No.' Grace shook her head emphatically. 'This is not your fault at all, Naomi. We don't know for certain how or why this occurs, but it usually happens in early pregnancy and there is nothing you could have done.'

Naomi knew better. This was where her baby was supposed to be safest, inside her. She was supposed to be nurturing it, allowing it to grow and develop. But her stupid body couldn't even do that properly.

She was usually so calm, so in control, of medical situations, even the most shocking events as an army nurse, but it was so very, terribly different being on the receiving end of them instead.

And this wasn't her area of medicine. Nor Bas's.

This was what it must be like for her patients and their families—this feeling of utter helplessness—when she was explaining things to them. The most wretched emotions washed around her.

It seemed that the excess of fluid was indicative of her baby having difficulty swallowing. Now, as she peered incredulously at the 'double bubble' of fluid in her unborn baby's ultrasound, she struggled to latch onto Grace's words.

'These dark spots here…' the doctor pointed '…and here, are what we call a double bubble. They show the baby's stomach and duodenum are fluid-filled, but as you can see there is no fluid further down the intestinal tract.'

'Which is indicative of duodenal atresia?' Bas stated, and Naomi found herself grateful for his calm, controlled presence.

He was helping her to find her way through when she knew that—without him—she might have felt even more overwhelmed than she already did now.

'So what now?' Bas continued. 'Is it surgery in utero?'

'Not necessarily. Many babies are operated on after birth.'

'So we just wait?' he demanded.

Grace was being as reassuring and positive as she would expect her to be. But even though she didn't know the woman as well as Bas did, she couldn't shake the impression that this was Grace's way of smoothing the way for more bad news.

'To correct the atresia, yes,' Grace confirmed. 'But we do need to perform a couple of other tests.'

Naomi's heart stopped hurtling and simply plummeted. She wanted to speak but she couldn't and was grateful when Bas stepped in again with quiet steadfastness.

'You're saying that duodenal atresia is associated with other birth abnormalities?'

'Not always.' Grace was trying to soften the blow but still, Naomi found she was bracing herself. She knew the language only too well. 'But we like to gather as much information as we can. Sometimes, duodenal atresia is the only complication, but it is possible that it may a heart-related birth defect or Trisomy 21 may be present.'

'What are the stats?' Bas demanded as Naomi could only stare hollowly at the screen.

'One in three babies with duodenal atresia also have Down's,' Grace confirmed. 'One or two in ten also suffer with congenital heart defects. So I'd like to send you for an amniocentesis, and then to our paediatric cardiologist for a foetal echocardiogram.'

'So much?' she whispered, her hand reaching instinctively to cover her belly.

As though that could somehow protect the innocent unborn baby inside her.

'The more informed we are, the better care plan

we can create for you, and the more the neonatologist will have to help care for your infant when they are born.' The doctor offered a bolstering smile. 'The prognosis is excellent for babies with properly diagnosed and treated isolated duodenal atresia.'

'When?' Bas demanded. 'When can these tests be carried out?'

'I'll book you slots as soon as possible,' Grace said.

'And the results?'

'The results might take a couple of days for the lab to process the amniocentesis.'

Naomi's mind lurched. Up to forty-eight hours of wondering and questions. Possibly more.

'What about the baby? Will it...? Will *she*...?' She stopped, looking to Grace for confirmation. Grace nodded. She was expecting a daughter. 'Will she be born normally?'

'With polyhydramnios, there is a high risk that the baby will be born early,' answered the doctor before turning back to Naomi. 'Hopefully, with the right care, we can get you to the thirty-seven-week mark at least. If the surgery isn't an emergency then it will most likely be carried out when your baby is two or three days old.'

'Presumably, in all cases the surgeon will open up the blocked end of the duodenum and connect it back up to the small intestine?' Bas clarified.

'Exactly. There are different subtypes of duodenal atresia, but the basic surgery remains unchanged. During surgery a feeding tube will also be passed from your baby's mouth, through the stomach and into the small intestine, which will be used for the first few weeks after the surgery.'

'Until the small intestine has healed.' Bas nodded, and Naomi knew it was his way of maintaining some semblance of control.

She struggled to do the same.

'And afterwards…' She stalled, her tongue feeling as though it didn't even fit her own mouth. 'After the operation, will she be able to feed? What I mean is…will she be able to feed from me?'

'It will usually take a couple of weeks for your baby's bowel to be able to tolerate milk feeds.' Grace smiled gently. 'Which is why we use the trans-anastomotic tube to bypass the join in the duodenum, to enable the feeds to start earlier. Once the recovery is under way, there would usually be no reason why you couldn't begin feeding your baby by either breast or bottle.'

'And what about long-term?' Grace asked. 'Should I—*we*—expect anything in the future?'

'I'd like to see the results of the amniocentesis and the echocardiogram before I make that assessment,' Grace reminded them softly. 'But, in the event of isolated duodenal atresia, the prognosis is good. There aren't usually any long-term effects.'

Naomi tried to nod, but none of it was what she wanted to hear. Then again, what parent would?

All she wanted was for Grace to tell her that it was all a mistake and that her baby was absolutely fine.

'Given the elevated risk of premature delivery with polyhydramnios,' Bas cut in, squeezing her hand, 'I presume we're talking additional rest, birth plans, monitoring the size of the stomach?'

Naomi felt her heart thump, and hang. There was something mounting in her that verged on the hysterical, but she wouldn't allow it to overtake her. She refused to. Her one consolation was that at every turn Bas was using pronouns like *us* and *we*.

He didn't leave her feeling as if she was alone in this. And she wondered why she wasn't more surprised.

'Easier said than done, I know—' Grace offered a rueful expression '—but try not to worry. Reduce stress as much as you can. I know you're in the middle of retraining, Naomi. But if you can take a break, or reduce the workload, try to do that.'

'I'll sort that. It won't be an issue,' growled Bas, staring at her as if daring her to defy him.

Any other time she might have. Even now a part of her felt as though she ought to argue her position and tell him that she couldn't just walk away from her career like that. But then her hand crept to her belly again.

Not every mother going through this would have the luxury of focussing solely on her baby. But if that was what Bas was offering to her, she'd be a fool not to take him up on it.

'I'll give you a moment to talk whilst I see if I can set up an echo and an amniocentesis,' Grace advised kindly as she headed for the door. 'Though I suspect Doctors Seddon and Rhodes will have left already, especially with the gala. We're probably looking at tomorrow at the earliest, if I tell them who it's for.'

She was looking directly at Bas as she spoke, and even as Naomi tried to shake her rebellious head he jerked his head up and down.

'Tell them.'

Grace bobbed her head in acknowledgement before sliding neatly out of the door.

And then it was just her and Bas.

'Thank you,' she managed stiffly, turning her neck to the side but unable to lift her head to look at him through the swirling jumble of thoughts. 'I'd like to go home now, and—'

'I think not.'

Naomi startled at his curt tone.

'I…we just established that I need to rest. For the baby…'

'And you will,' Bas agreed tersely. 'But not there. Not a ridiculous bus-ride away. And not in those godawful flats. Not with my child.'

'Those godawful flats are my home. They're where my grandmother and sister are. My family.'

'You aren't carrying their baby,' he ground out. 'You're carrying mine. And that means you're coming home with me.'

'No…' she tried to argue, but a traitorous part of

her wanted nothing more than to do exactly what he was telling her.

'My apartment is around the corner, not somewhere in the back of beyond. It's bigger, and more modern, and it's closer to the hospital for coming in for the tests.'

'What am I supposed to tell my family?'

'Tell them that you're with your baby's father,' Bas told her sharply. 'You know, the one with whom you've pretended to be in a relationship all these months? Tell them you're moving into your new home.'

'But it isn't my home,' she cried.

He eyed her coldly.

'At least, from now until this baby comes out, safely, consider my home yours.'

'You're crazy. They won't believe that. They—'

'Then convince them—I don't care how. I recommend you don't push me on this, Naomi. You won't like my reaction.'

And as much as Naomi wanted to stand her ground, and appear independent, she found herself staying silent. A Leila far more grown-up than she used to be would be on hand to look after her grandmother, after all, and they'd probably both be relieved to know she was being looked after for once in her life.

Maybe Bas was right, and she *did* need him to look out for her. For their baby. She clearly wasn't able to. The scan earlier had given her a huge shock.

How could she not have known something wasn't right with her own baby? In her own way, she must be as bad a mother as her own had turned out to be.

How had she not realised that premature delivery could be a complication? She wasn't sure if that made her a worse mother-to-be, or doctor. Either way, it left her feeling somehow more lacking than ever.

Dully, she bobbed her head.

'Fine.'

Because what other choice was there? This thing was serious, and there was nothing she could do but wait.

And hope.

Naomi woke the following morning in an unfamiliar bed, the unusual sound of nothing around her, the morning sun cascading light onto the empty pillow beside her—and with it, a fresh sense of hope.

She was in Bas's guest suite—a beautifully furnished white and grey minimalist space, the footprint of which was likely bigger than that of her entire apartment back home. And strangely she felt lighter than she had in quite some months.

Her baby had every chance of being okay. The echocardiogram—taken once Bas had placed a call and brought Dr Rhodes hurrying back to the hospital—had been gloriously clear, with no signs of defects or abnormalities.

There was still the amniocentesis to go, and then

the wait for the results. But all in all, she was feeling far more positive than yesterday.

No mother wanted to think of their baby needing surgery the moment it was born, but if the duodenal atresia was the only concern—and everything pointed to that being the most likely outcome—then the overall prognosis was good.

And the fact that Dr Rhodes and Grace, had been so happy to give their time for Bas—a surgeon who had apparently given up his days off and free time for them on several occasions, from what she dimly recalled—said a surprising amount about the man who was father to her baby.

But now a different question was beginning to gnaw away at Naomi. From the way Bas and Grace interacted, there was clearly something more to their relationship than simply colleagues. A sort of…unspoken closeness.

For her baby's sake, she ought to understand that better.

Throwing back the covers and swinging her legs over the side of the bed, Naomi caught sight of a small rucksack across the room. One that looked suspiciously like Leila's old college bag. Curiously, she walked over to unzip it.

A selection of her clothes, packed neatly and efficiently. And with them the dress that Leila had been diligently sewing all week, claiming it was her latest college assignment, and refusing to let Naomi see it until it was finished. Carefully extracting the garment and unrolling it, she held it up.

It had to be one of the prettiest dresses Naomi thought she'd seen. Her favourite colour, and a fabric that Naomi loved. But even better than that, the slight shaping to it told her instantly that it was a flattering maternity style. Her eyes pricked.

Trust Leila to have thought of everything.

And how had Bas got it from her sister? The faster she dressed and found him, the faster she could get her answers.

Padding through to what was clearly her own private en suite bathroom—but which was bigger than her living room back home—she stepped into an expansive shower, all gleaming glass and polished stone tiles, and luxuriated in the water jets that powered out of the walls, cleaning her body until she felt brand new.

A few minutes later, the stunning dress swirling around her legs, and her damp curls tied up in an easy pineapple on her head, she poked her head out of her room before moving slowly along the corridor.

She hadn't even been sure what she'd been expecting from his apartment—something that was part dark bachelor pad and part kinky dungeon, perhaps, but this place wasn't either.

Instead, the apartment was light and airy, with white walls, and slick, clean lines of shimmering glass and gleaming metal. Modern, yet without feeling cold, or sterile. Not somewhere she could ever imagine a sticky-fingered child, she thought with a pang. She'd rather have a house, with a play-room, and a garden—but it certainly suited Bas.

She took her time looking around. The main living areas, a study with another incredible view over the city, the guest suite, which she had slept in—and a hasty dash past the master suite where she didn't care to think of Bas sleeping—before finally returning to the vast open-plan living room and kitchen where he was, of all things, making her a cup of tea. Naturally from a minimalist boiling water tap, no mere kettle for Basilius Jansen.

'Find what you were looking for?' he asked, mildly.

She was glad he wouldn't be able to read the flush of heat that rushed to her cheeks.

'Sorry?' She feigned innocence.

'A mistress locked away? A bawdy S & M room perhaps? I suppose I should be offended that the mother of my baby thinks so little of me.'

His voice wasn't friendly, exactly. But some of the ice from the previous day seemed to have thawed, if only a little. Or perhaps that was just what she wanted to think. She frowned, a little of her earlier positivity dissipating.

'Perhaps that's because you appear to actively encourage people to think the worst of you. At least, when it comes to your personal life, you do.'

'People will think whatever they want to think,'

he countered, in a tone that warned her that particular line of conversation was over.

No matter, there were always a hundred other questions all jostling for position in her head. The question was where to start?

In the end, she plumped for the first one that reached her tongue.

'What are we doing here, Bas?' She wasn't sure how she managed to keep her tone so even. So neutral.

'Doing where? In my apartment? I told you yesterday, I'm making sure the baby you're carrying— *my daughter*—is being looked after as well as she possibly can be.'

'Only less than twenty-four hours ago, you were questioning whether you were actually the father of this baby. Now you've dragged me here, to your penthouse, because I'm not doing a proper job of taking care of *your* baby. I'm not the enemy here, Bas.'

Her voice cracked on the last part, and she could have kicked herself.

'Are you not?' he asked quietly. Dangerously.

'No,' she managed as calmly as she could. 'I'm not.'

Inside, she felt like a churning mess. Not least because she was still trying to work out how things had changed so quickly from the sense of relief they'd both felt emerging from the echocardiogram. How *Bas* had changed from that uneasy truce they'd seemed to have forged.

'It is time to decide what we are going to do.'

'What we're going to do?' she echoed.

'About the baby. My daughter. We need a solution.'

'*Our* daughter,' she said, before realising she'd meant to say anything at all. 'And I have a solution, thank you very much.

Stalking wordlessly around the vast living room, Bas flung himself into a brown leather armchair and stretched his long, muscular legs out in front of him with unexpected insouciance.

Being alone with Bas—in his penthouse—was feeling more and more taut by the minute, and it didn't matter how many times she told herself it was just the nerves of the situation, a part of her didn't quite believe it.

He, meanwhile, merely waved a hand casually in the air.

'Sit down.'

She narrowed her eyes at him. The best she could manage, all things given.

'I'm not a dog you can train to perform tricks.'

'Asking you to sit down is hardly that,' he snorted.

She arched one eyebrow in an attempt to convey the impression that she was actually irritated. With him.

'You didn't *ask*.'

He held her eyes a moment longer.

'Sit down, *please*,' he amended grudgingly, his eyes not leaving Naomi's.

For a moment, she didn't move. And then, she offered a delicate sniff as she moved to the straight-back dining chairs around the glass and resin table. No need to risk looking ungainly dropping into those sprawling plaid and leather sofas, which were so buttery soft that they looked as though they'd cost about the same as her actual apartment.

Pulling the chair out, she moved back, startled.

'There's a cat under the table.'

'Probably,' Bas replied evenly. 'There are underfloor heating pipes running under there, and he likes to lie on them. So long as he isn't on the table or chairs, I leave him be.'

'He's yours?'

Bas eyed her sharply.

'Is that so shocking?'

'Well, frankly…yes.' It suggested all manner of things about Bas that she would have preferred not to know. 'How long have you owned him? What's his name? How did you even come to own him?'

'I didn't realise having a cat was such a crime.'

Naomi wrinkled her nose.

'It isn't.'

'And yet, I feel distinctly interrogated by such a barrage of questions. Where should I even start? How about here? His name is Sonny, I'd say he owns me more than I own him, and I got him when he was a kitten some eleven years ago.'

'Eleven years?' Naomi exclaimed before she could stop herself.

That was longer than some people's relationships lasted. Even some marriages.

'Grace and I were walking down a canal tow-path, back from the hospital, when I saw a plastic bag moving. When I went to investigate, I found two freezing, sodden kittens—three, actually, but one was clearly dead. Grace took one, I took the other, and he's been with me ever since.'

Naomi opened her mouth, trying to find the right words.

'Oh.'

It suddenly seemed significant that he'd had that cat for over a decade. It meant that she could no longer tell herself that Bas Jansen didn't understand the meaning of commitment. He'd committed to a damned cat. For over a decade.

Suddenly, it seemed possible that he could commit to their daughter. If that was what he wanted to do.

She wasn't sure how she felt about that. But before she could consider it in any greater detail, Bas started speaking again.

'What exactly was it that you expected from me, Naomi?' he demanded, without further preamble.

She fought away the flustered feeling that stole over her and lifted her head as high as she could.

'I already told you. I didn't expect anything. I *don't* expect anything.'

'Is that why you hadn't intended to tell me about her?'

The question walloped into Naomi, winding her. It took her a moment to catch her breath.

'I fully intended to tell you about her,' she choked out at length.

'When?' he pushed relentlessly. 'When she was born? When she became a teenager? When she turned twenty-one?'

Naomi bit her lip.

'Before she was born.'

'And I'm supposed to simply believe that? You're twenty weeks pregnant, Naomi. You've known for months, you've had scans, you even told your family. But you didn't think to tell me? The father?'

Naomi dropped her head. Of all the things she'd done in her life, that was certainly her most shameful. She watched her fingers whiten as her fists clenched and unclenched in her lap. And then—she couldn't have said where it came from—a calmness overtook her and she lifted her head back up to meet Bas's glower.

'You're right, and I'm sorry. I just…didn't know how to tell you. Or even if you'd want to know. Your reputation…' She tailed off with a shrug.

'These are your excuses?'

She shook her head vehemently.

'They aren't meant to be excuses, so much as my attempt to explain what went through my head. I was afraid you might think I'd done it deliberately for your money, or connections. I was even afraid that I would lose my bursary once your father discovered I was pregnant. And so, I kept putting it off until I could find the right way, the right time, to tell you.'

'Did you really think there could be a *right time*?' Bas demanded as she gazed at him miserably.

'No, I guess not. And the simple truth is that you had a right to know. So I'm sorry. More sorry than you can ever know.'

Was it just her imagination, or was there a thawing in the room?

'Say I choose to believe you. Say you were going to tell me…' he lifted his hand into the air '…at some point before the birth. You're claiming that you would have done it because it was "the right thing to do"?'

'Yes.' Naomi sat straight, determined not to betray any of the turmoil she felt inside. But she didn't speak.

'But you don't want anything from me? Not a thing? How very *decent* of you.'

And still, his tone lacked the bitter edge of before. A drumbeat pounded hard in her chest, and it sounded very much like the rhythm of optimism.

'I think we've just established that, so far, I've been anything but decent. But it's true. We had a one-night stand—'

'Not even,' he cut in.

'And my falling pregnant was an accident. But for me, it's turned out to be a happy one. I want this child, and I get to choose to do that. But if I hadn't wanted her, I would have got to choose that, too. As the woman, I get to make that choice. You don't. So the very least I can do is allow you to walk away without recriminations.'

'This is my child, Naomi. I can't just walk away.' He didn't need to launch himself up for her to read how tightly coiled he was. 'I'm not the monster you clearly believe me to be.'

She gawked at him in shock.

'I don't think you're a monster at all. How could I? You took me for that scan. You ensured I got the tests I needed. You even enlisted my sister's help to get me clothes when you insisted I came here.'

'Because your idea of looking after yourself would have been going back to full-time work, which you got to by sitting on a bus or two for hours every day; and living in a flat which I highly doubt is big enough for three, let alone three and a baby. I'd hazard a guess that you and your sister still have to share a room. Am I right?'

'No,' she answered, truthfully.

He wasn't convinced.

'Am I right, Naomi?'

She clamped her jaw shut, forcing herself to maintain eye contact. But, eventually, she couldn't stop her eyes from sliding away.

'I sleep on a sofa bed in the living room,' she muttered.

Something dark shifted in his eyes right then, and Naomi realised that, no matter how casual he appeared to be, he was filled with just as much pent up emotion as she was.

'And then you were going to introduce a baby into that mix? I would hardly call that a solution.'

'Plenty of people manage with less.'

She had intended to sound placating, but the words came out more defensively. Little wonder that Bas leaned forward instantly.

'Not any child of mine,' he told her. 'Just as no child of mine will grow up without a father.'

A wiser woman would have paid heed to the dangerous note in his voice. Naomi regretted that she had never thought of herself as all that wise.

'So what exactly are you proposing we should do?' she challenged. 'Enlighten me, please.'

'I am merely telling you that I will be present in her life. I will be there whenever she needs me.'

Which meant *what*, precisely? For a moment, Naomi considered that Bas might not even knew himself what he wanted.

But the next second she dismissed such a notion. Of course he would have a plan. He was Bas, he always had a plan. It didn't mean she would like it.

'Listen.' She cleared her throat, trying to get her point in before he could voice his. 'I appreciate all you've done, and that you're trying to do the right thing now. But let me spare you by saying that you don't need to. In fact, I don't want you to.'

'Say that again. You don't want me to be a part of my child's life?'

Her stomach churned, but she fought to quell it.

'No, I don't want you dipping in and out of our daughter's life. Or mine, for that matter. It isn't an option.'

She pretended the words didn't scrape her raw inside. Because to admit that might mean she had to admit a few other home truths.

'We agree on that much,' he bit out. 'I don't intend to dip out of anything.'

She tried again.

'What I mean is, you might say that now out of some misguided notion of taking responsibility, but the reality isn't the same. You'll grow tired of it.'

'And you know me well enough to make this assessment, do you?'

Again, his words wielded a dangerous edge. And again, she chose to blandly ignore it.

'I'm not judging, but surely you can see that it's inevitable?' She forced her mouth into a semblance of an understanding smile, though it near killed her. 'You'll grow bored, or resentful. Probably both. With luck, it will be before our baby even knows who you are, so she won't notice your absence. But I think we both know that it would be better not to have that around a baby. You live your life, and I'll live mine. That can be our arrangement.'

'Enough!'

He didn't shout. He didn't even raise his voice. Yet it was clear to Naomi that something inside Bas had detonated. And so she fell instantly silent.

'That is not how things will be,' he murmured quietly. Too quietly.

'It's for the best. You're free, Bas. I release you of all responsibility.'

He glowered at her, his eyes boring into her so hard that she was sure they would leave bruises. Not that she would have been alone in her pain, she could see how tightly his jaw was locked.

'You misjudge me completely if you think that is any kind of an acceptable response,' he ground out.

She lifted one shoulder as delicately as she could.

'Perhaps, but is it any wonder? You're a closed book, Bas. I hardly think you're going to open up to me.'

This time, his eyes narrowed on her.

'If you have questions, maybe you should try simply asking them instead of going through this pantomime.'

'Maybe.' She inhaled deeply. 'But what would be the point? You'd never answer them.'

'Try me.'

Whatever she'd expected, it hadn't been that. Naomi caught her breath, trying to work out if she had the courage to ask all the questions she wanted to. Any other time, she likely wouldn't have but then, any other time, she wouldn't have even been here.

And she wasn't asking for herself; she was asking for her daughter.

Exhaling slowly, silently, Naomi lifted her gaze back to Baz. It was now or never.

'Okay,' she heard herself ask. 'Then tell me what your relationship to Grace Henley is. And explain what she meant on the phone yesterday when she said you could be a good father because *"You're not him. And you sure as hell aren't her".*'

Bas didn't answer. He simply went still. The air in the room pulled taut, wrapping itself tightly around her and squeezing as though it would force all the air out of her lungs. Out of the room.

And she willed him to speak, to explain and open himself up to her in some way. Anything that might help her to feel as though they were more equal partners in this, instead of her and her pregnancy being an issue that he had to deal with. A problem to solve.

Because she didn't need him to *solve* anything. She'd been dealing with problems on her own for as long as she could remember. She didn't want rescuing. Wasn't this one of the reasons she'd found it so difficult to tell him she was pregnant in the first place?

Still, she silently urged him to talk. But he didn't.

And then, without warning, the mobile phone he'd spun so casually onto the coffee table blipped an alert, breaking the moment as he reached out to read the message.

In one smooth movement, Bas launched himself to his feet, tipping back his mug and finishing his drink in one mouthful. Naomi couldn't say she was surprised when he strode across the room away from her, to set the empty cup on the gleaming granite worktop.

His voice totally emotionless he said, 'For the baby's sake, I suggest you try to rest today, the amniocentesis is scheduled for midday tomorrow.'

'Midday,' she echoed, thoughts of Bas forgotten as everything felt as though it was crashing in on her at once. 'That was the message that just came through?'

'Be ready here by half-past eleven. I'll have my driver, Phillip, collect you.'

'We aren't…that is…you don't want to…'

She'd never stuttered before in her life, and she didn't like that she was starting now.

Bas eyed her coolly.

'You were quite clear that you wanted to be seen with me as little as possible and, unlike last night, the hospital will be heaving in the middle of the day.'

'Right,' she muttered, half in a daze.

Bas continued as though she hadn't spoken.

'Also, I still have patients, and I have a packed schedule today and rounds to do in the morning. But I will be in Seddon's office at the designated time tomorrow.'

And then, just like that, he was gone. Leaving Naomi all alone in a room that was possibly the most expensive, pristine living area she'd ever seen in her life. But which didn't feel remotely like home.

CHAPTER SEVEN

THROWING HIS GOWN and gloves into the bin, and checking his hands for stains, Bas pushed through the OR doors to de-scrub.

Jimi's surgery had gone smoothly. A subcutaneous mastectomy with a direct resection of the glandular tissue.

Bas eyed his patient through the glass.

The peri-areolar approach with liposuction had been textbook, and Bas was confident that he'd achieved good contour regularity with accurate symmetry. Only time would tell whether Jimi would have numbness or loss of sensation. Or whether there would be any tissue-shedding as a result of blood loss.

It was as good an outcome as Bas could have hoped for. He ought to be happier.

But his mind—now that it no longer had the complex surgery to distract it—was already shifting back to Naomi. But not the amniocentesis from the previous day, so much as the conversation he'd walked out on the day before that.

The last time he'd been home in two days. Instead, he'd been hiding out here in the hospital, using his patients as his cover, and taking on additional on-call duties—all to avoid returning back home. Back to where Naomi was.

All because he hadn't—wouldn't, couldn't—answer the questions she had asked him.

He'd challenged her to ask whatever she wanted, with the assurance that he would answer—his opportunity to make her trust him. But then she'd asked one of the few questions he simply hadn't been expecting, and he'd cut and run, using the hospital and his patients as an excuse for not returning in some thirty-odd hours. And using the on-call room to catch some shut-eye.

The irony didn't escape him.

He scrubbed angrily at his skin, wondering what his next step ought to be. He felt wrong-footed, and it wasn't a state of being that he was accustomed to. He didn't find it suited him well.

'How are you doing?'

Whipping his head around, Bas cast his friend Grace an even stare.

'The surgery went well.'

'I didn't mean the surgery.' She moved to stand near him. 'I meant you.'

He wasn't sure he was going to answer, until he heard his own dry voice.

'You mean, aside from the fact that my unborn baby is going to need surgery mere days after she's born?'

'I'm so sorry,' Grace told him sincerely. 'I can only imagine what you and Naomi are going through.'

A strange lump lodged in Bas's throat. He told himself not to be so emotional.

'Thanks. No amniocentesis results?'

'Not yet.' She pulled a face. 'Seddon put a rush on it, but it still takes time—you know that.'

He grunted.

Knowing how things worked didn't necessarily make it any easier to wait, though.

'Do you and Naomi know what you're going to do yet?' Grace asked. 'In terms of raising the baby, I mean?'

'Do you mean how involved am I going to be?' he demanded. 'It's my child, Grace. Or do you think the same as Naomi? That I'll just *dip in and out of their lives*?'

Grace didn't take the bait. He hadn't really expected her to.

In many ways, she was like Naomi. Calm. Even-tempered. The main difference was that Grace was his friend, whilst Naomi was the woman whose face had—inconceivably—haunted his dreams at night, these past months. And whose body he'd tasted so thoroughly, so indulgently, that he thought he could have identified her blindfolded.

With an effort, he dragged his mind back to what Grace was saying.'

'Is that what Naomi thinks?' she asked. 'That you wouldn't be dependable? Then again, she doesn't know you. You hide the real you well, so I guess you can see her side of it, can't you?'

'Not really,' he replied tersely as his friend cast him a sidelong look. He might have known she wouldn't let him get away with it. 'She asked me what you meant when you talked about me not being like Magnus. Or my mother.'

Grace didn't answer immediately. Instead, she waited as though she expected him to say more.

'You didn't answer, did you?' She sighed eventually.

'I don't see that it's any of her business.'

'You can hear the absurdity of your comment, right?' Grace prodded softly. 'Naomi is the mother of your unborn child. Like it or not, she has a right to hear a little about your past, and the way it shaped you.'

'Does she?' countered Bas. 'It isn't as though we've chosen to be together. If it weren't for this pregnancy, we probably wouldn't have even spoken again.'

And yet, even as he said the words, it felt like a punch to the gut. As though something inside him fundamentally disagreed with such an assertion.

Still, he wasn't prepared for Grace's reaction.

'Wouldn't you?' she asked, carefully.

'What's that supposed to mean?'

'It means that I don't think I've ever seen you act quite the way you did around Naomi,' Grace shrugged. 'And it isn't just that she's pregnant, or that you were both dealing with the news that no parent-to-be wants to hear, because I noticed even before the scan.'

'You're imagining things,' Bas scoffed.

But it took more effort than it should have.

'I don't think so. There was just something… different, about the way you were around her. The softer side of Bas that I usually only see when you and I are alone. I think you like her, Bas. And I think you think so, too.'

He wanted to say something scornful. Or laugh at the suggestion, at the very least. But he couldn't, though he couldn't explain why.'

'How did the gala go?' he demanded instead, stepping off the foot tap and drying his hands.

Grace paused, presumably wanting to say something more. But then she seemed to dismiss it.

'The gala went very smoothly,' she assured him. 'People asked after you, naturally, but I just said you were caught up in a case here. In any case, a record amount of money was raised, and a good night was had by all.'

It wasn't the question he'd really been asking. Given the other parts of his life that were currently blowing up, he just wanted to hear that his brother, Henrik, hadn't turned up to make his presence known.

It made his voice sharper than Bas would have preferred.

'Nothing else to tell?'

Grace hesitated again, and this time there was no mistaking the wariness in her gaze.

'Are you talking about the new doctor on your exchange programme?'

It took everything in Bas not to give into a sudden urge to pound the wall. Violence had always been his stepfather's go-to, never his own, but in that moment Bas felt positively murderous.

Henrik had actually dared to go to the gala.

'He was there?' Bas choked out. 'You met him?'

'I did.' Her voice sounded odd, tight, but he couldn't focus on that now. 'Is there some reason I shouldn't have?'

Bas's mind raced.

'He was actually there? He had the bloody audacity? And you didn't think to call me?' snarled Bas. 'You didn't think to even mention it?'

'I rather thought you had enough going on,' Grace managed jerkily. 'Don't you?'

'Not more important than Henrik turning up,' Bas retorted icily.

And Grace blinked quickly. A myriad unspoken thoughts chased across her face.

'Wait. *Henrik?*' she echoed slowly. 'You mean Rik?'

'Rik?'

'Dr Rik Magnusson, the new surgeon.'

The red haze seemed to turn a darker crimson.

'That's what he's calling himself?' Bas snorted.

A few days ago, he would have single-mindedly tracked his so-called brother down to whatever rock he was hiding under, and he would have sent the traitor back to where he'd come from.

Instead, he felt torn in two. All he kept thinking

of was Naomi, back at his apartment, without even the distraction of surgery to keep her mind off the impending amniocentesis results. And suddenly, Bas didn't have either the time or inclination for Henrik, right now.

Grace, it seemed, was still chasing to keep up.

'When you say Henrik, you don't mean…?' She stopped awkwardly. 'But he called himself Rik. And surely he would be a Jansen?'

'My father's name is Magnus,' Bas thrust his hands into his pockets in an effort to conceal his clenched fists. Though he couldn't be sure whether it was at Rik, or at the time this unwelcome conversation was taking up. 'Presumably, he thinks he's clever calling himself Magnusson. And shortening Henrik to Rik.'

'Perhaps he's trying to be discreet,' she managed in an anguished tone. 'Maybe he's trying not to cause a scene.'

If only that were true.

'If he doesn't want a scene, then he shouldn't have come here. He should have stayed the hell away, just as he has done these past thirty years. Just as he ought to have done when I didn't answer any of his letters.'

'Rik wrote to you?'

There was something so demanding in the question that it pulled Bas up short. He eyed his friend a little closer. Her pulse was hammering in her neck, as though she was upset.

Or guilty.

'Rik?' he demanded harshly. 'You're acquainted with him?'

The silence stretched out too long.

'I didn't know who he was,' Grace cried at last.

The implication was clear. Bas felt cold dismay bubble up inside him.

'You had sex with him?' he said coldly. 'Of all the people in this hospital, in this county, with whom you could have had sex, you chose my brother?'

'How could I have known?' Grace raked a hand through her hair.

'I asked you to go in my place and to look out for anything unusual. Anyone who was there who shouldn't be.'

For a long moment, they stood watching each other. And then Grace's panic began to die down, and she eyed him critically.

'And from that, I was supposed to know you meant your brother?'

Bas gritted his teeth. 'Anyone unusual, Grace.'

'I couldn't possibly have known that meant the brother you haven't seen in almost thirty years. I couldn't possibly have concluded that the stranger I happened to meet—the perfectly…normal man, who called himself Rik and was a surgeon like so many people at that medical ball—was someone *unusual*.'

Bas snorted his disdain.

'You think you *happened* to meet him? That it

was a coincidence that he bumped into you—the person I'm closest to?'

He watched as she registered what he was saying. Then paled. She shook her head.

'You're saying he sought me out deliberately?' she whispered, her words jagged.

And even through his anger, Bas felt a pang a guilt at how the truth would hurt Grace. And he hated Henrik even more for putting him in such a position. But he knew Grace, she was strong, and fiercely independent, and he wouldn't be much of a friend if he let her believe that his brother hadn't known exactly who she was when he'd seduced her.

And then something else sneaked through him, creeping so stealthily that he almost missed it at first.

If Henrik was underhanded enough to sleep with Grace in order to glean information about him, what would his excuse for a brother do if he found about Naomi? He needed to find her. To…well, not protect her precisely, but…

Bas faltered. What did he want to do if not protect Naomi? She was the mother of his child, after all.

He shut down the voice in his head that asked if that was all she was to him.

Things were so fragile between the two of them. So delicately balanced. The last thing he needed was Henrik crashing in with whatever manipulative power game he was here to play out.

This was his baby they were talking about. He couldn't risk losing her because Naomi decided his family was so twisted and spiteful that she didn't want to have anything to do with him.

However sickeningly true that might be.

'I have to go,' he told Grace. 'But you need to meet up with Henrik again.'

She cast him a horrified glance.

'What? *No!*'

'Yes.' He nodded grimly. 'Whatever he's doing here, whatever he's up to, I need to know.'

Perhaps he should have paid more heed to Henrik's letters, but it was too late now. Now, it was all about damage limitation. Just like the most acute trauma patients who came into his OR.

'Wait, you want me to spy on Henrik?' Grace looked appalled. 'I can't. No. If you want to know why Henrik's here, Bas, you're going to have to speak to him.'

He could read the discomfort in every line of her body, and a sliver of guilt ran through him. But he couldn't give into it. He played his trump card.

'Please, Grace, I'm asking you as my friend. Whatever Henrik is doing here, it won't be good. But I have to concentrate on Naomi right now. She has to be my priority. My baby has to be my main focus.'

'Bas…' Grace bit her lip. 'What you're asking…'

'I'm not asking you to sleep with him again, for pity's sake,' Bas told her, as he realised what she thought. 'I'm just asking you to occupy him. Distract him. Maybe show him around the hospital. Take him on a tour of the city.'

'Show him around…' she echoed uncertainly.

But she wasn't saying no any more, and he took that as a good sign.

A thought struck him.

'You could even ask him to take my place in the hospital fete this year.'

'You really want Rik… Henrik, to get involved in the charitable side of the hospital?'

'Not particularly.' Bas gritted his teeth. 'But you know how long the prep work takes, between repairing the stalls and giving the tired ones a fresh lick of paint. And then there's the manning of them. It takes time. All of which I could be spending with Naomi this year.'

'I don't know, Bas.' Grace pursed her lips. Her distaste for the whole thing was evident.

And maybe he was throwing her under the bus a little, but he really needed her to do this. Because whilst Henrik was focussed on Grace, he wasn't focussed on Naomi.

He just had to apply a little more pressure—as unpalatable as that was. For Naomi and his baby's sake.

'You slept with my brother, Grace. I think you owe me.'

She opened her mouth as if she was going to

argue some more and then, abruptly, she closed it again.

'Okay,' she muttered, so quietly that he could barely hear her. 'Okay, I'll do it. I'll try to keep him distracted. But there's a time limit, Bas. I'll give you a week.'

'A month,' he negotiated bleakly.

'A fortnight. So you'd better do the right thing by Naomi, Bas. And you'd better agree on your solution quickly.'

Bas offered his friend a grim nod and made his way to the door.

'Agreed. And, Grace...' He stopped briefly to turn back to her. 'Thank you.'

Naomi knew he was there without even seeing him.

It could have been the buzz in the corridor outside, or the way her colleagues suddenly, subtly changed. But really, it was the way her body came alive—the little things, from the tiny hairs on the back of her neck, to the goosebumps on her lower calves.

Or perhaps it was just the fact that she'd been half expecting him.

But she refused to turn to him, concentrating instead on the consultant standing with her in the small doctors' room along the corridor from her patient's bay.

'He presented a year ago with lower back pain, and it has been getting progressively worse. We diagnosed compressed nerves in the lumbar region and we've tried NSAIDs, corticosteroids and TENS relief. Physiotherapy has been a non-starter.'

Quickly and efficiently, she ran the consultant through the case, presenting her notes and explaining her conclusions. All the while ignoring Bas, though she could feel his eyes boring into her back.

Then, eventually, as the consultant left she finally allowed herself to turn.

'What do you think you're doing?'

Sucking in a steadying breath, Naomi plastered a neutral expression on her face and turned around.

'I'm on shift,' she told him mildly. 'Just like you.'

He took her elbow—not entirely roughly—and bundled her out of the door and into the nearest empty room which—given how hectic the hospital was already—was no mean feat.

Part of her wondered if these vacant spaces materialised just for him. He wielded that much power in the place that she wouldn't have been shocked.

But that didn't mean he had authority over her.

'You're supposed to be resting.'

His tone might seem mild enough, but she wasn't fooled. She cranked her smile up a notch.

'I rested and was monitored for an hour yesterday,' she told him. 'As you well know, since you were the one doing the monitoring, right alongside Dr Seddon. And then you walked me to the car park where your driver took me home, as per your instruction.'

'And yet here you are now. In work,' he pointed out. 'Not—as you can see—still at the penthouse.'

She could dodge, as a wiser woman might have done. Or she could bite the proverbial bullet and tell him exactly what she thought. Naomi barely thought twice.

'Because I decided that I didn't particularly want to sit around there—as magnificent as your home is—staring at four walls and driving myself slightly crazy while I think about these results. I did enough of that yesterday—which I might have told you, had you deigned to return last night.'

'I was working.'

'How convenient.' It was all she could do to sound breezy. 'So, you dragged me from my own home, where at least I would have had company—my grandmother and sister to distract me—and installed me in a place where I am basically isolated from anyone and anything.'

'I would hardly say isolated. Your family are free to visit. Provided that I am not there.'

'How generous of you.' She fought back the bitterness from her voice. 'Especially after you invited me to ask you whatever questions I needed to, but when I did you actually got up and left.'

'Because you need to rest.' At least he had the decency to look mildly guilty. 'Just as you need to rest now.'

'I need to work,' she exclaimed crossly. 'To be useful. And this place—whilst better off than most public hospitals thanks to also being home to the Jansen wing—is at capacity and always down on staff. Do you really think anyone asked twice when I turned up as an extra working doctor?'

Bas let out a low rumble of disapproval.

'And how, precisely, did you get in to work today? Did you take a bus? Don't tell me you walked.'

'If I had done, it wouldn't have been an issue. Your building is practically around the corner from this place—I can only imagine how much that must have cost, even without it being the penthouse. But no, for the record, I asked Phillip to drive me in.'

'Phillip?' Bas exclaimed irritably. 'He should have let me know the minute you called. Scratch that, he should never have agreed to drive you here in the first place.'

'Phillip is your driver, not your security guard.' Naomi actually laughed. 'And I've no doubt he would have tried to contact you, but I imagine you were already in surgery. Didn't you tell me that you had surgeries to catch up on, since you pushed them in order to be with me for the test?'

Bas looked furious.

'I never begrudged that.'

'I never suggested that you did,' she told him, deliberately sweetly. 'I'm merely pointing out likely scenarios to stop you from doing something impulsive like sacking poor Phillip. Have you checked your phone?'

'Not yet.'

'Ah. Well, there you go. Now…' ducking around him, she headed for the door '…if you don't mind, I'm sure there will already be a new patient waiting out there for me to see.'

She had no idea how Bas made it to the door before her.

'Absolutely not.'

'Bas…'

'You may be completely insensible to the seriousness of what's going on, Naomi, but I am not. And you are carrying my child.'

'I'm perfectly aware of that fact.' She dipped her head. 'And, no, I am not *insensible* to the seriousness of my baby's situation. But I do not wish to sit in a prison—albeit a luxuriously expensive one—with nothing to do all day but torture myself with everything that could go wrong.'

'This is not about—' began Bas.

But she cut him off.

'I've had the scan. I've done the tests. The echocardiogram was clear, and I rested all day yesterday after the amniocentesis, the results of which are yet to be determined. You've already ensured that I will get a battery of scans, and if I should develop polyhydramnios, and there is any suggestion of risk of early delivery, then I will go on full bed rest. Until then, I fully intend to keep working as my Jansen Bursary expects.'

His glare could have skewered her to the spot.

It might have done, had she been a lesser woman. She squared her shoulders.

'Or are you the kind of person who feels that, because of their position of power, they have the right to dictate every aspect of the other person's life?'

'This isn't about me exerting power over you, Naomi. This is about me ensuring our baby is as safe as it can be.'

'And you think I'm not?' Her cool exterior began to crumble. 'You think I'm not terrified? You think the worst scenarios aren't lurking in the back of my mind? I just want a shift where I can push them aside and focus on other people's problems. Maybe try to solve a few of them, because, heaven knows, I can't solve this for myself.'

Bas eyed her wordlessly, but he refused to budge. For a moment, she thought he was going to fight her some more.

And the worst of it was that she didn't have the strength to fight back. The last few days' events had drained her, mentally and physically. More than she'd been prepared to admit.

'How about a compromise?' he said gruffly, after the silence between them had begun to fray.

She eyed him archly.

'You'll give up your work if I give up mine?'

He glared at her.

'Where are you working today?'

'Here.' She gestured to the corridor outside, and the ward they were on.

'Not Resus? Or A & E?' he demanded. 'Not Plastics?'

'No. Just here.'

He stared at her, and she wasn't quite sure how long passed.

'Fine, have it your way, Naomi.' He ultimately blew out a harsh breath. 'At least until the results of the amnio come through. But if there is any indication whatsoever of a problem, or if you get tired, or experience anything at all out of the ordinary, you get a message to me. I don't care what I'm doing, I don't care if I'm in surgery, you get a message through. Understand?'

She hadn't expected him to capitulate so readily. Blinking, Naomi offered him a brief bob of her head.

'I understand.'

'And once your shift finishes, you go to Phillip and he will take you straight home. Straight home, Naomi.'

'Straight…home,' she confirmed, as strange as that sounded to her.

'Then, all right,' Bas grunted out grudgingly. 'I shall see you back there tonight.'

And Naomi pretended that a traitorous part of her wasn't looking forward to that moment a little too much.

CHAPTER EIGHT

NAOMI HEARD THE exclusive penthouse lift ping its forewarning of someone's arrival a few moments before Bas actually appeared at the front door. Certainly long enough for her to have vacated her position on the settee, taking her book and retreating to the relative security of her guest suite.

But she didn't. She refused to run and hide. Bas was the one who had insisted she moved in with him—however long that was meant to last—and so now he was going to have to deal with her presence.

Contrary to what she'd told Bas earlier that day, she'd ended up on Paediatric A&E after all—treating a baby with an abnormally slow heart-rate, an eight-year-old who had shoved a building block in his ear, and another who had stuffed a button up her nose. None of it had fazed her.

But now, she now sat tensely, the words on the page swimming before her eyes each time she attempted to read, as Bas stepped into the penthouse.

'You had a good shift?' he asked, dropping his keys and his bag before making his way to a polished oak and resin cabinet, and retrieving two glasses.

'I did.' It was impossible not to sound formal. 'It was...what I needed.'

Truth be told, it had been an incredible relief

to spend the day working. As though everything were normal.

'Good.'

He didn't sound as if he thought it was good. Then again, she couldn't tell what he sounded like. But then, how could she? When all was said and done, she barely knew the man.

The father of her unborn child.

She watched him prepare a drink—two drinks—and then cross over the room to set a sparkling water down in front of her, and a brandy down in front of himself. But he still caught her off-guard when he started to speak.

'You worried that I would want to dip in and out of your life, and that of our daughter. You asked me what Grace Henley meant to me. And you wanted to know what she meant by me being nothing like my father. So which part do you want me to answer first?'

Slowly, Naomi turned her book over on her lap, trying to stop that tremor in her hands. Working on smoothing the look of shock that was surely clouding her face.

'Start wherever you think the beginning is.' She swallowed.

Bas reached for his tumbler of brandy and took a long pull.

'My brother is here. In the UK. At Thorncroft.'

It was all she could do not to clear out her ears. She couldn't possibly have heard that correctly.

'Your…brother?'

Setting the crystalware back down, Bas offered a grim nod.

'Up until I was seven, I lived in Sweden with my brother, a sorry excuse for a wannabe singer—my mother—and the fist-flailing two-bit musician we were led to believe was our father.'

He stopped as if waiting for her to speak, but Naomi just wanted to hear what he had to say. Besides, she wouldn't have known what to answer if she tried.

'One day, after he'd sent my brother Henrik flying across the room and head first into the wall—this time for interrupting his quiet time when it was me who'd asked our mother whether I had any clean underwear for school—I told my teacher what our father was doing to us. Child Welfare came and investigated.'

'And they discovered Magnus Jansen was really your father, and sent you to him?' she asked, unable to stop herself.

'No.' He jerked his head bitterly. 'My mother told them that I was an angry child who had a propensity for lying. When they presented her with medical records, she convinced them that I was the one who had caused the injuries to my brother because I flew into rages.'

'They believed her?' Naomi couldn't disguise her reaction.

'My mother has always been very…convincing.

She told them that it had started when I'd discovered that my real father had abandoned us all, and that I resented my stepfather, even though he was a good man who had taken us all on despite the fact that Henrik and I weren't his. I can still remember my brother and I standing in that room, and the shock I felt at hearing about our real parentage for the first time.'

'What about your brother? When he told them what really happened, how could they not believe two of you?'

Bas felt his face twist into something ugly, and there was nothing he could do to stop it.

'Henrik sided with our mother. Usually, she protected him, and it was me who got hit. Their relationship was…closer. And so when my mother said that I was the one who had been lying, he backed her up.'

'Bas…'

'He betrayed me.'

Naomi hesitated. It was humbling that Bas was confiding his truth in her—*her*—and she desperately wanted to say the right thing. To help. But something niggled at her, and she couldn't swallow back her words, even though she knew she ran the risk of alienating him.

She had to be true to herself.

'I can't imagine how that must have felt for you, as a seven-year-old boy,' she began falteringly. 'But, Bas, Henrik was only seven, too. Could he have thought he was pouring oil onto troubled waters when he said what he did? Do you believe he could have known what the consequences would be?'

'By lying?' Bas snapped.

But, for a split second, there had been a hesitation. An acknowledgement of what she was saying.

'Ah,' she said quietly. 'I see it now. You blame Henrik because it's easier for you to do that and hate him, than for you to have faced all those years torn away from the brother you loved.'

Bas didn't reply, but his jaw locked tightly—the pulse flickering angrily at its base. It was the only answer she needed.

'Is it still too painful, even now, to forgive your brother?' she pressed softly. 'Or is it that it's been so long that you no longer know *how* to forgive him?'

He glowered at her—silent and imperial—and she wondered if she hadn't perhaps gone too far. And then, just as she was about to give up thinking he would confide anything more in her, he worked his jaw as if trying to loosen it.

'I have no wish to try,' he bit out. 'Once it was over, my mother screamed at me that I was an ungrateful and vindictive child—I won't bore you with the words she actually used—and she told me that I should be more respectful of the man who had taken me in as his son, especially when I was such a piece of work. And then she told me that I was going to live with my real father.'

'With Magnus,' Naomi breathed. 'It must have been a shock to find out he had a son.'

'Two sons,' Bas bit out. 'Henrik and I are twins. Fraternal—to be exact. And no, it wasn't a shock. He was aware that we were supposed to have been our mother's meal ticket to marrying an up-and-coming surgeon.'

'Magnus had known about you?'

'Yes, he'd known. But he'd paid my mother off—handsomely, apparently, though she'd blown through it all in those first few years—to never again trouble him with two babies he didn't want.'

'Oh.'

'She drove me to the airport, stuck me on a flight, and told me to take a taxi when I landed at the airport and that Magnus would pay the fare.'

'My God.'

'Magnus was livid, of course. He tried to contact her, to get me sent back, but when she threatened to go to the press and tell them that the great Magnus Jansen was an absent father unless he took me on and sent her another generous pay-off, he complied. Only this time, he had a pack of lawyers to tie her into an airtight contract.'

Bas took another pull of his drink before he continued.

'After that, he told me that having a kid around his neck was the last thing he'd ever needed, but that it was his obligation to give me a home and a decent education. He also said that it was my obligation to repay him by proving myself one day, and at least becoming a "halfway decent" surgeon, worthy of the Jansen name.'

Naomi shifted in her seat. She wanted to cross the room, and put her arms around him, make him feel the love she was beginning to think he'd never known. But she suspected that Bas wouldn't thank her for it. To the contrary, she could well imagine him pushing her away.

Was this why he was the way he was? The hospital playboy, never forming attachments, never allowing himself to get close to anyone.

'So you've been living with your father ever since? And your brother has been living with… your mother?'

'It was always going to be a better fit for him there. Henrik was always her favourite. Like I said, we aren't identical twins, so whilst we might look similar in terms of body type, he has more of our mother's features, whilst I look like Magnus—the man who she believes got her pregnant and walked away. According to her, Magnus is the devil who ruined her life. And, unbeknownst to me, I'd had his look about me since birth.'

'Ah,' she offered, uncertain what else to say.

'Henrik was also the one through whom she'd been able to live vicariously. She always said she was an undiscovered star. The singer who had never caught her big break. Since Henrik could sing and I definitely can't, she always intended for him to become the superstar she felt she'd been robbed of being.'

'So now he's here? At Thorncroft?' She wasn't sure she followed.

'He is.' Bas barked out a laugh. A hollow, scraping sound. 'But he isn't some singing sensation. He's a surgeon.'

'A surgeon?'

'A plastic surgeon.'

'Like you.' Naomi gasped before she could bite it back.

Though she managed not to add, *And like Magnus*.

'Exactly like me,' Bas confirmed bitterly.

'I…see.'

Though she wasn't sure she did. Not really. Was it really a bad thing that his brother had chosen to be like him rather than like their mother, given all that Bas had said?

Was it, somehow, a compliment to Bas?

'And if that wasn't enough,' he ground out unexpectedly, 'I discovered today that he sought out Grace at the medical ball the other night and seduced her.'

Ah. Grace.

Naomi tried valiantly to swallow back the questions jumbling inside her. But it proved too much.

'What exactly is Grace, to you, Bas?'

His stare practically skewered her.

'I've heard rumours…' Naomi continued, stiffly. The fact was that she'd only heard them that day, when she'd begun asking discreetly around the hospital. But once she'd asked, she could hardly believe she hadn't heard them before.

According to everyone she'd asked, Grace wasn't just a brilliant doctor, but she was the suspected reason that Bas never dated the same woman twice. According to the hospital grapevine—not that she usually liked to put much stock into idle rumour—Grace was Bas's soulmate. The one who got away.

Even now, as she thought about it, a ripple ran through Naomi that couldn't possibly have been jealousy. And no matter how she thrust it aside, it still danced there, on the periphery of her mind.

And she hated herself for it because she had no right to be upset. Bas owed her nothing. They weren't a couple—she was just the woman who'd been foolish enough to fall pregnant by him.

She came back to, to realise that Bas was staring grimly at her.

'That's all they are,' he bit out. 'Rumours. Nothing more. We've been good friends since med school.'

'But that's it?' Naomi couldn't silence her tongue. 'I'm not stirring up anything by going to scans with her when I'm carrying your baby?'

She studiously ignored those odd internal undulations as he peered at her. Rather too closely. She didn't care much for that gleam in his eyes, either—the one that said he could read her uncharacteristic thoughts. And that he liked them.

The last thing Bas needed was for her to send his already stratospheric ego into the ionosphere.

He scratched his chin, as though deciding what to tell her.

'I'm aware that there are those who consider me self-indulgent, with an addiction to the finer things in life. Grace claims that it's actually my form of self-flagellation. She calls it my personally appointed hell, an adult version of the one in which she thinks I've been languishing for the better part of three decades.'

Naomi cocked her head to one side.

'And what do you think?'

'I think that I've always found her theory laughable.'

He didn't add the words *until now*. But she thought she heard them, all the same.

'And what does Grace think of…this situation?'

Bas cast her a shrewd look.

'Do you want to know what she thinks of this situation? Or what she thinks of you?'

And Naomi didn't like it that he seemed to read her so easily.

She wrinkled her nose. Clearly, he wasn't going to tell her, anyway.

'Forget I said anything.'

'Surely that isn't jealousy I can see, Dr Fox?' He frowned. 'I can't say I think it suits you.'

'Of course I'm not jealous.' She bristled, ignoring the little voice in her head branding her a liar.

'I just want to know that the woman who is going to be operating on my newborn baby isn't going to be contending with her own feelings about the fact that you're the father.'

The black look in Bas's eyes—unmistakeable anger—was hardly settling. But it was the hint of guilt that really wheedled its way under her skin. Surely guilt could mean only one thing?

'There is nothing between Grace and me,' he bit out icily instead. 'But let me make one thing absolutely clear, Grace would never, never jeopardise the life of the baby. She is an incredible surgeon, and a good friend. She would never ever be unprofessional. Do I make myself clear?'

And it was perhaps the vehement way that he defended his so-called 'just a friend' that felt, to Naomi, like the most damning indictment of all.

If Grace really was the one who got away, then there was no way Naomi intended to compete with that.

Hadn't she learned, many years ago, never to settle for second-best? Hadn't she promised herself that she would never again be anyone's second choice?

The most terrifying part was that, for a moment there with Bas, she had let herself be lulled into believing that she wasn't his second choice.

That she and the baby genuinely mattered to him.

She wouldn't be so foolish as to make that mistake again.

* * *

Bas checked his phone for the tenth time in as many minutes.

The results of the amniocentesis were due today, and it had taken him these past couple of days to realise that the wait was practically driving him insane.

He could only imagine how hard Naomi was finding it.

He'd lost count of the number of times he'd had to wait for tests to come back on patients; he'd schooled them on the importance of the tests being done right, and he'd always believed he'd had good empathy for the people under his care, as well as their fraught families.

It turned out he hadn't understood anywhere near as well as he'd thought he had. It felt very, very different when *he* was the one feeling powerless. Useless.

All those pat little phrases he had as a surgeon— the ones that enabled him to express sympathy without actually having to experience the same loss as a family, because how could he have done his job if he'd allowed himself to feel *exactly* what they felt?—now seemed so hollow and empty.

The row—if his eruption could be called that— with Naomi the previous evening had to be testament to that. A result of the shock he'd felt to realise that he'd opened up to her more than he had anyone in the past.

Ever.

And that included Grace.

There was something about Naomi that made him want to tell her things he'd spent the past few decades trying to bury. And he couldn't explain it.

Or didn't want to.

So here he was throwing himself into work—the one thing that was meant to be his solace. The one thing that he could do to make a difference. It was the thing that he understood best.

Yet all he could think about was Naomi, and if she was okay. How she was coping with this interminable wait. Up until that last part of the previous evening, it had felt as though they had grown a little closer.

As though maybe they actually could find a resolution for the situation in which they now found themselves. Because, clearly, living together long term wasn't remotely a viable option. But when he tried to imagine when it would be best for Naomi to leave—he found it impossible.

The idea of being apart from his daughter felt... wrong. And yet he didn't doubt that the more contact he would have in her life, the more he would eventually mess her up.

Just as his own parents had done to him.

How could it be that Naomi, who hadn't had either parent in her life, seemed so much more together and in control than he thought he would ever feel?

Being a surgeon was one thing. But being a father...? It held a terror he would never before have believed.

The worst of it was that, for the first time in his career, it was as though he was going through the motions. He was doing all the right things, saying all the right things, but all he could think about was Naomi.

Automatically, his hand reached for his mobile, punching in the keys to speed-dial her to ensure that she was okay, and that she was resting the way she needed to be. As if they really were some kind of couple. As if she would want him to be that solicitous.

Bas stopped, his finger hovering over the button to make the call, and it took him all his self-control to cancel it and drop the mobile back in his pocket.

The original agreement for Naomi to move in with him had been one born out of practicality—out of a desire to have Naomi close to the hospital after discovering that their unborn baby had a serious medical condition.

It hadn't been something they'd discussed—it had just happened. But now the initial shock had worn off, he felt it was time to start making plans. To discuss what would happen once their daughter was actually here.

In his head, the logical move would be for Naomi and their baby to remain here, so that their daughter could have the family and emotional security that had been so lacking in his own upbringing. It was a chance to offer his child more than he'd had.

But was he fooling himself to think that he was capable of that?

More than that, would it open the door to Naomi imagining that something more was going on? He was fairly sure she hadn't thought that a few days ago, but since then the lines had begun to get blurred. And he wasn't sure he could pinpoint why.

Bas was still pondering the matter when his pager went off, calling him downstairs.

'Talk to me,' Bas stated as he hurried into A & E.

'Fifty-five-year-old male with subtotal hand amputation following accident with a circular saw. He's in bay five.'

'Another DIY accident,' Bas noted grimly, cutting a path across the room.

Accidents involving home owners and electric saws were all too common, and they were rarely straightforward. He could only hope that this one wasn't too serious.

Especially when he'd heard that Henrik was on call somewhere in the hospital.

The last thing he wanted was some run-in with his long-lost twin brother.

'Someone paged me,' he announced himself as he reached the bay, his attention immediately drawn to the man—ashen and blood-soaked—lying on the trolley.

One glance at the hand told him that this was

more than a little accident. The message he'd been given had stated it was a subtotal hand amputation, but that didn't begin to convey the fact that the man's extremity had been almost severed in two places and was only still attached thanks to the faintest sliver of skin and bone.

He cursed inwardly whilst maintaining his usual poker face. It was going to take some skilled work if he was going to stand a chance of saving this man's hand. Many surgeons might have considered it unsalvageable, but Bas had sewn hands and feet to groins before now in an attempt to save a dying extremity.

The most crucial initial step was going to be to get him into a surgery to repair as much as possible and establish a good blood and nerve supply to the fingers. Or what fingers remained.

'Book an OR,' he murmured to the ward sister as he watched the patient being wheeled away to be prepped for surgery.

'It's booked.'

Bas stopped, an iciness stealing over him at the sound of the voice, the faintest Swedish lilt. If the hospital had crashed down around him, Bas couldn't have felt any more razed.

He certainly wasn't sure how he managed to turn around.

'Henrik,' he bit out. 'What the hell are you doing here?'

Staring at his brother was like staring at a ghost.

Bas had thought he'd imagined this moment in enough detail to know what he was going to do. And say. But he hadn't foreseen the gamut of emotions that would run through him the moment he looked into those familiar blue eyes again.

It was a body-blow. A reminder of a time when he and his brother had been so close that he'd thought nothing could ever come between them. A time when he'd never dreamed Henrik would ever betray him. A time of innocence—no, of gullibility.

How dearly he'd paid for such naivety.

'It is the Jansen exchange programme.' The faint Swedish lilt and a set of painfully familiar eyes cast Bas to stone on the spot. He couldn't have jerked away if he'd tried. 'I have been writing to you three times.'

Slowly, slowly, Bas's breath seeped back into his lungs. He worked his jaw a few times.

'I am aware. It landed me with the task of having to throw them in the trash where they belong.' If he hadn't known it was himself speaking, Bas didn't think he would have known his own voice. 'My mistake—what I really meant to say was, get away from my case.'

'The way I am to keep away from Grace?'

Bas eyeballed him.

'Grace is a grown woman. She makes her own decisions. And I never told her to stay away from you.'

'No. You merely told her that I have targeted her because I knew you two were friends.'

'I can't imagine Grace told you that,' Bas said levelly.

Though when put like that, it sounded even worse than he remembered.

'Of course not. She is loyal to you. But she asked me, and I knew it had come from you.'

'Perhaps so.' Bas wasn't about to apologise. 'But it wasn't a lie, was it?'

'I went to that medical ball to talk to you, Basilius. I did not know who Grace was when I first spoke to her that night.'

Bas eyed his brother shrewdly.

'But you knew who she was when you slept with her. Didn't you?'

And it was odd, wasn't it, that even after all this time he didn't need Henrik to respond in order for him to know the answer to that question?

'As I thought,' Bas spat out, disgusted.

He wasn't prepared for the look that shadowed his brother's face.

'What is Grace to you, Basilius? Do you love her?'

Bas stopped, taken aback.

'Grace is a friend,' he rasped. 'Nothing more. Has she not told you that?'

Henrik eyed him in frank assessment.

'That's exactly what she told me. But I'm not a fool, brother. I know you sent her to watch me. What is your saying? *Keep your enemies close?*'

'Something like that,' Bas murmured.

'So, I shall ask you again, do you care for her, Basilius? Because I think I might, and I am willing to fight for her.'

And he looked so sincere that if Bas hadn't known his brother's tricks first hand, even he might have believed Henrik.

'You're not capable of fighting for her. Or anyone.' Bas snorted, making no attempt to conceal his disdain. 'You don't know what love is, Henrik. Neither of us do. The only thing we know is that sick, twisted version of love that we learned from *them*.'

He didn't need to say their names for his brother to know he was talking about their mother and the man she'd passed off as their father for years.

But then something flashed across his brother's face. Something that looked incomprehensibly like...sadness.

'Is that what you really believe?'

'It's what I know.' Bas glowered. 'She might have favoured you, but it didn't make her idea of love any less dangerous. There were always strings attached to her affection.'

'And what about Mrs P? And Bertie?' Henrik asked quietly. 'Were there always strings attached to their love? Or have you forgotten them, Basilius?'

But Bas couldn't answer. He thought his brain might have shut down.

Mrs P. Even the mere name was enough to send emotions cascading through him, throwing open memories as if they were coffins, uncovered in a dark crypt where he'd forgotten he'd even buried them.

Mrs P, the kind, lovely cook, and her husband, Bertie, who had worked in the mechanics garage down the road from their home. How could he ever, ever have forgotten them, and the way the pair had treated him and Henrik like the children they'd never had?

With kindness. And care. And *love*.

They'd been the stable family that he and Henrik had never had. And then, one day, they'd simply left.

'They deserted us,' he bit out.

Because they too had seen something fundamentally unlikeable in him. And they'd rejected him like everyone else.

'They didn't leave,' Henrik told him softly. 'We left. We went from that suburban house to that flat in the city. Don't you remember?'

Bas shook his head tersely. He didn't. Or, at least, he hadn't. Now, all of a sudden, something was beginning to unfurl in the back of his mind. Hazy and dark, but there nonetheless.

'Mother was always so jealous of them,' Henrik said jerkily. 'The way we always used to go to them first for things. Don't you recall running into their kitchen on the way home from school and they'd be waiting to hear about our day, with milk and home-baked fairy cakes? Sometimes, we got to decorate them.'

Bas blinked. He couldn't say he remembered exactly, but things were beginning to take shape. As though his past was slowly, *slowly* pulling into focus.

How had he forgotten all of this?

Something pricked at the backs of Bas's eyes and he blinked it back viciously. *No.* It couldn't possibly be tears.

No weakness. Wasn't that what Magnus had always taught him?

Impulsively, he shoved the alarming tangle of memories back into their boxes. But they were too messy, and they wouldn't go back properly. They kept spilling out.

Bas folded his arms over his chest and forced his head up.

'Is that why you called me for a consultation on this patient?' Cold, precise, his voice did a remarkable job of disguising the storm of emotions that raged inside him.

And Henrik paused. Faltered. Then offered an almost imperceptible shake of his head.

Whatever conversation the two of them hadn't quite been having, it was not over. And they both knew it.

'I did not call for a consultation.'

'I was paged,' Bas gritted out.

'I called for another surgeon.' His brother shrugged.

'I could not have known that would be you. It is an urgent case.'

And even though he didn't believe Henrik, Bas realised he couldn't dwell on it. There wasn't time. There was a patient who needed urgent care and, like it or not, he now had no choice but to work with his brother to save the patient's hand.

'Fine,' he growled at length. 'Run me through it.'

Henrik dipped his head in assent and swiped his screen to his notes before passing the tablet over.

'Preliminary tests have been run, and a CT. The sooner I operate, the better, but it's likely to run late into the night. Two surgeons working together will make it a faster surgery for the patient. Less time under anaesthetic means less stress on the patient.'

It made sense. He'd worked on relatively similar injuries before, and the operation could run to ten, twelve, even fifteen hours. Two surgeons would mean that one surgeon could be harvesting grafts from lower limbs whilst the other worked on the hand. And Henrik had a point: the less time the patient was under anaesthesia, the better for them.

The choices ran through Bas's head.

The thought of spending hours effectively locked in an operating room with no way to avoid his brother certainly didn't appeal. And yet...the surgeon side of him was drawn to the case. How could he pass up this operation to someone else?

How could he choose not to be part of the case

when he knew he could well be this patient's best hope?

'I've seen cases like this before, but this is probably one of the worst cases I've seen,' Bas stated in a clipped tone, which was nonetheless too quiet to be heard by the patient, or his family. 'I suggest you pass this case to me to take lead. I can bring in a surgeon on my team to assist.'

Henrik fixed him with a steady gaze that was all too familiar. He had seen it in himself any time he looked in the mirror.

'If you don't feel able to assist me…' his brother's voice was equally low, but firm '…then by all means send another member of your team. However, I have completed several of these procedures in the past. The last case I worked on involved cutting a flap of skin from the groin to embed my patient's hand, to allow the skin to grow and provide new covering.'

Bas schooled his features. His brother's words virtually mirrored everything he'd been thinking when he'd first seen the patient and it was simultaneously galling and…something he didn't care to examine further.

'You've harvested veins and nerve grafts from the foot and forearm, to reconstruct the hand?'

'And joined tendons and arteries, yes,' Henrik confirmed. 'As I know you have. So it is up to you to choose whether to work with me on this patient, or not. But right now, I really need to get him into surgery. The sooner I can re-establish blood supply, the better his recovery is likely to be. Are you joining me, or sending someone else?'

It galled him that Henrik was right. And apparently more skilled than he'd wanted to believe. Bas couldn't remember the last time he'd had to be second surgeon to another plastic guy. But this was Henrik's patient and, personal feelings aside, there was no way the surgeon in him could walk away.

'I've worked on these microsurgical repairs many times before,' Bas stated. 'It's quite draining. You'll need to be good.'

'As will you.'

Bas met Henrik's level gaze. He refused to be the first one to blink.

'You have to be realistic about his prognosis. This will never be a normal hand, but, with time and effort, physio can help him regain strength.'

'I made his family clear that even holding a pen will be good progress,' Henrik agreed. 'He'll need multiple surgeries over the next few months, even years.'

'In time perhaps we can go for a power grip.'

'In time,' Henrik agreed. 'Either way, I must take him in and begin now. I need a decision, Basilius. Can you work with me? Or no?'

Bas paused for one fraction of a moment longer before dipping his head in tacit acquiescence. Then, with a signal from Henrik to the rest of the team, the bay once again became a flurry of activity as they prepped to bring the patient up to Theatre.

They had hours of surgery ahead of them, and Bas couldn't stop himself from wondering how he would ever get through it with the brother he had vowed never to have any contact with, for the rest of his life.

Slowly, methodically, they began, until at last, fourteen hours later, they found themselves peeling off their gowns and gloves, after a successful operation. And Bas thought he should probably say something.

'Good surgery,' he muttered, rolling up his gown and gloves and hurling them into the medical waste bin, before marching through the doors of the surgical suite to scrub out, leaving his brother to finish up his debriefing.

'Very good,' Henrik agreed, joining him at last. 'Would you care to join me in telling the family?'

It was on the tip of Bas's tongue to agree, but seeing a message on his phone stopped him. Finishing his sterilisation routine, he reached for it.

The results of the amniocentesis.

Without a backward glance, Bas hurried out of the room. It was Henrik's patient. Let his brother deal with the family himself.

He had to find Naomi and tell her. Not to mention trying to rationalise those memories that Henrik had so unexpectedly raked up.

CHAPTER NINE

BAS TRIED TELLING himself that he wasn't panicking, that he never panicked. But as he moved slickly through the gears, his car speeding down the dark deserted city streets, he began to feel something rising inside him which felt a lot like he imagined panic to feel.

Naomi was supposed to have been in the cafeteria, waiting for him. But when he'd got there only to learn that that she'd already left for home, it had been terrifying.

Was she tired? Ill? Was something wrong?

It was all he could do not to smash the speed limit as he hurtled around corners. But he was a surgeon. He'd seen too many accidents, put too many broken bodies back together, and faced too many devastated, grieving family members.

But at last, he was home. Stepping into his penthouse lift and willing it to hoist him up to his floor faster.

He saw her the moment he crashed through the door, standing on the decked balcony, her hands on the cool metal balustrade as she looked down to the city below. Hauling the doors open, he stepped through, and just about restrained himself from hurrying over.

'Naomi, is something wrong?'

'I'm fine. I just thought the fresh air might help to clear my head.'

She didn't turn her head to look at him but her voice carried through the air assuredly as though she'd sensed his approach. Yet the sensation that shot through him only bemused him all the more.

'Is that your apology for not being in the hospital cafeteria where I instructed you to wait for me?'

It wasn't what he'd intended to say. He wasn't even sure where it had come from.

This time, she did turn her head.

'Were you expecting me to sit obediently like a trained animal, waiting for you? If so, I suggest you get yourself a dog. Preferably a working one, like a border collie, or a German shepherd.'

Her dry tone licked at him in ways he didn't care to analyse further. He told himself it was resentment, but he wasn't sure he was convinced.

'The results of the amniocentesis are back,' he told her gravely.

She gripped the railing tighter.

'What do they say?'

'See for yourself.' He held out his phone and, stiffly, she turned to take it.

A few seconds later, she stumbled and fell against him. Half choking, half sobbing.

'Oh, thank God.'

'We should discuss how we proceed from here.' At least his voice sounded cool. Controlled. Even if he felt anything but.

For several seconds, she didn't speak. She merely continued her laugh-crying. And then, slowly, she regained control and turned back to the balustrade.

'*We* don't need to discuss anything,' Naomi managed quietly. 'I told you about the baby because it was the right thing to do—and, again, I'm grateful for yesterday—but I don't need you. *We* don't need you. You're free, Bas. Why must we discuss this any more than that?'

'Because we're not discussing some inanimate object here,' he exploded. 'That's my *child* you're carrying. Which makes her my responsibility.'

She flattened her hands on the metal balustrade.

'But it doesn't *have* to,' she murmured. 'That's what I'm trying to tell you. I understand this isn't what you bargained for. I get to choose whether I want this baby or not, and for the record I do want it. You don't get to make that decision for me. So I'm saying that I won't blame you if you walk away.'

'How very magnanimous of you.'

He wasn't sure how he was keeping his temper in check. It was hammering through every inch of his body, threatening to punch its way out.

Did she really think he'd thank her for pushing him out of his baby's life?

'You think I'm being high-handed here.' She met his eyes and, this time, she didn't let her gaze slide away. 'But I believe you'll thank me for it later. You might be prepared to do what you think is the honourable thing, and step up as a father, but deep down you don't want the responsibility of a kid weighing you down.'

'And you do?'

'It might not have been what I planned, but I intend to be there every step of the way. I *want* this baby, Bas. I'm ready for her. But you can't say the same.'

'I'm as ready as you are,' he managed evenly as Naomi snorted delicately.

'That certainly isn't true. You expect me—us—to return here. To a less than baby-friendly pristine penthouse of metal and glass.'

'As opposed to that cramped place that wasn't big enough for three of you, let alone one of you having a baby.'

'At least it was a home. It was cosy, and it was real. This is a bachelor pad with white walls, and marble tiling, and shiny metal. A place which boasts unparalleled views of the city through sparklingly clean, floor-to-ceiling glass. How long is a child going to last in a place like this?'

'You're objecting because of where I live? One of the most prestigious postcodes in the city?'

'You're an intelligent man, Bas,' she countered softly. 'You understand what I'm saying. You didn't even think about that side of it, did you?'

He hadn't. And it galled him to admit it, even to himself.

'So where, precisely, would you live, Naomi? If you could live anywhere in this city?'

And he couldn't have said what rattled through him as he watched a faraway look enter her eyes—the corners of her mouth pulling up a fraction.

'It's a cliché, I know, but I always wanted a place in the country, with rambling roses, and a pretty fence. It wouldn't have to be fancy, just homely. A house for a family. A home. With a garden, and a room where my child could play. A place where there might be a few sticky fingers, or pencil marks, but, more than that, there would be lots of laughter.'

'A place like that would be totally incompatible with working at Thorncroft,' he dismissed. 'That's an impractical fantasy, whilst I'm talking about realities.'

'I know the reality, Bas.' Her eyes sparked, and he thought he preferred that fire to the wistfulness of before. 'I'm the one who was telling you about reality. I'm the one who wants this child and will be there for her.'

'And I intend to be there every step of the way, too.'

'How? By dropping in and out of her life when the demands of your career and/or your love life allow?' She shook her head. 'I want my baby to grow up knowing it's loved, wholly and unconditionally. By me. I want it to feel like the most important thing in my life. I don't want it growing up thinking that it is, at best, a mild inconvenience. Or, at worst, unloved. Believe me, I know how that feels.'

She stopped sharply, biting her lip as though she hadn't intended to say anything. But Bas was already caught up with his own fury.

'Do you imagine that you have the monopoly on unwanted feelings?' he demanded furiously. 'That you have been the only child in the world not to be wanted by their parents?'

'You're the son of Magnus Jansen.' Her brow pulled tightly together, as though she was irritated by him. 'Your father taught you everything about becoming a surgeon.'

'It didn't mean he wanted me. You think I have a reputation as a playboy, but my father was King Lothario. If he wasn't at the hospital, he was with a woman. Practically a different one every night.'

'Yet he still taught you all he could. Imagine a kid like me, with a mother who dumped my sister and me for the next man who took an interest. Social services visited us so many times that my grandmother had no choice in the end but to take us in.'

'I thought you said she loved you. That she was a good woman.'

'She did love us. But that didn't stop me from feeling second choice. It's all relative, isn't it?' Naomi shrugged. 'My mother never wanted me so my grandmother *had* to take me on. And then take Leila on, when the same thing happened to her.'

'I understand,' he murmured.

But Naomi seemed caught up in her own thoughts.

'My grandmother kept a safe roof over our heads, but I was the one who cooked, and cleaned. She didn't have much choice, of course. She'd been a cleaner all her life and had no savings. The meagre pension she received didn't stretch far when it came to feeding and clothing two growing kids.'

He didn't answer. What was there to say?

As private a person as he'd always prided himself on being, it was nothing to the way Naomi pulled her secrets around her like a warm cloak on a cold winter's night.

Or a shield.

They stood in silence for so long, and he was beginning to think she wasn't going to tell him anything more, when she began talking again.

'She bought what she could from second-hand shops, and some of it wasn't bad. But the other kids always knew, anyway. Always last season's stuff, or older. And every time I got laughed at, or my schoolbooks knocked to the ground, it made me feel second rate. Not good enough.'

'Which is why I don't want that for our baby.' He didn't intend to sound so abrasive, but he didn't apologise when it did, either. 'I felt that, too, Naomi. But our daughter never has to.'

She watched him, her breathing shallow. And he got the sense she was trying to compose herself.

That made two of them, then. Although he didn't intend to let her know it.

'I know that,' she managed at length. 'I don't want my child to go through what I went through, either. And that's why I let myself get drawn in by your suggestion that I move in with you. That we try to raise this baby together. But it won't work.'

'It will work,' he told her firmly.

'No.' She shook her head fiercely, and he wondered if she knew how attractive a quality he found it. 'It doesn't. It doesn't make the slightest bit of sense. And neither does the fact that I was so desperate to have a family that I leapt at what you offered. But it isn't real, is it? It's just an illusion. And what happens when that illusion shatters?'

Bas pulled his jaw tight.

He let his gaze wander over her. He wondered if she knew how often her hands cradled that baby bump, as though she could protect it from the worst this world had to throw at it. He considered all the things he might say to sway her back to his original plan. But he didn't let himself think about what she was saying.

Because he didn't think he could answer her questions.

Or *would.*

'It won't shatter,' he bit out. 'You and I will ensure it doesn't. Regardless of the circumstances, we both want what's best for this baby. She will have every opportunity she needs. I'll make sure of that.'

And finally, Naomi met his gaze. Eye to eye.

'Financially, I don't doubt you,' she told him earnestly. 'But in terms of being in her life, day in and day out…? I don't think you can do that.'

'Then you don't know me,' he cut her off coldly.

'Bas…'

'I've been understanding up until now, Naomi,' he growled. 'But let's be crystal clear here, I will not be shut out of this child's life because *you* had a poor childhood and you've suddenly realised that you don't want to trust anyone but yourself.'

'It is *not* because I had a poor childhood. But that does give me some true perspective.'

'You don't even know what kind of perspective I have,' interrupted Bas. 'But this child will have two parents who love and cherish them. No matter the personal cost.'

Naomi threw her hands into the air.

'But that's exactly my point. There won't be a personal cost for me. I *want* this child.'

It was crazy. He understood the logic of what she was saying, but, no matter how earnest she was, he couldn't reconcile it. The words made sense in his head, but then they mixed with this *thing* swirling around his chest, and everything became confused.

'I will be recognised as this baby's father. I will be present in its life. I won't relinquish that just because you're afraid I'll walk away. And I won't keep having this conversation with you. We already settled this, a week ago, when you accepted moving here with me.'

She blinked rapidly.

'I know…but I was wrong. I accepted for all the wrong reasons. I accepted because I was scared of doing this alone. But I shouldn't be. I can do this. I know I can. So I'm offering you the *out* now.'

'Have you ever considered that you're making these decisions based on your own fear of letting go of control?' he demanded.

'What?' She snapped her head around. 'No. This isn't about control. This is about wanting the best for my baby.'

'Which you seem to think doesn't include a father who actively wants to be there for his child.'

He recognised that defiant tilt of her chin.

'I've told you—this isn't about being there some of the time. This is about the day-in-day-out banality of being a parent. You live your life at full throttle, Bas. The two don't mix. At least, not well.'

'For all intents and purposes, you've been the one running your family all these years,' he continued, as though she hadn't spoken at all. 'I'm just suggesting that maybe the idea of relinquishing control, or even just sharing it, terrifies you.'

'No…' She shook her head.

'Let's be absolutely clear, Naomi. I am this baby's father, and I will not let you sideline me.'

She opened her mouth to argue. He could read it

in every line of her lush body which still—against all appropriateness—called to him as if she were some siren and he were a sailor enthralled in her song.

'I'd think very carefully about what you say, or do, next,' he cautioned, though a part of him wondered who he was really warning. Naomi, or himself?

He watched, unduly fascinated as she drew in several steadying breaths.

'I think we're going around in circles here,' she offered at last.

'I couldn't agree more, which is why I have a solution,' he replied, and though he knew he had said the words, he had no idea where they'd come from.

She eyed him uncertainly.

'What kind of solution?'

'You're worried about coming to rely on me only for me to abandon you, so you're trying to draw a line between us from the start.'

She inclined her head but didn't answer.

'So we make it so you don't fear me walking away.'

'And how do we do that?' She laughed scornfully. 'Some legal contract drawn up by any of your highly experienced team of lawyers?'

He didn't laugh.

'Of a sort.' He shrugged. And then heard himself say, 'I'm talking about a marriage contract.'

'A marriage contract?'

She gaped at him as though he was half mad. Possibly he was.

He certainly had no idea where *that* suggestion had come from.

'What does that even mean?' she choked out, when he didn't answer.

'It means marriage, Naomi.' The words were still coming out of his mouth despite the fact they appeared to have completely bypassed his brain.

He had no idea what he was saying. Yet, at the same time, it all seemed so logical. So practical.

'No…you don't mean it?'

And Bas felt it spoke volumes that her words came out a little more like a breathy question than the incredulous refusal that he believed she'd intended.

'You're proposing marriage?' she added when he didn't respond.

'I thought I was quite clear,' he answered, his voice calm. No mean feat given that he didn't even understand what he was doing.

Naomi sucked in another sharp breath, though it did little to settle the manic fluttering in her chest. He struggled to drag his gaze away.

'You can't be serious. It's an insane suggestion.'

If he wasn't very much mistaken, she looked altogether too tempted to say *yes*. A sense of victory rolled through him.

'I disagree.' He sounded far too calm. 'Your main concern is coming to rely on me, only for me to walk out. You don't want to feel second-rate. Not enough.'

'I don't want my child—our daughter—to feel that way,' she corrected.

He wondered if she knew that slight tremor in her voice gave her away.

'That's why you want to take it on all on your own from the start, right?' he demanded. 'You believed that, at least that way, you would already be geared up to do this alone.'

She stared at him mutely, and he knew then that he had her.

'You will marry me, Naomi. You will marry me because you are carrying my child and because I will not have my child growing up as I did. Or, indeed, as you did. She deserves better.'

'Bas…'

'It's our responsibility, as the people who have brought her into this world, to do everything we can to give her the childhood we never had. I know that's how you feel, too.'

Marriage would be his punishment for breaking all his rules, and for wanting Naomi too much.

And if a part of him wondered why his punishment didn't feel more…punitive, then no one else needed to know it but him.

CHAPTER TEN

THIS WAS ABSOLUTELY CRAZY.

A hundred objections tore through Naomi's head, but the one thing she couldn't shake was quite how Bas seemed to be able to read her so easily.

As if he really *got* her when no one else ever had done in the past.

She thrust the notion aside, and tried valiantly to remind herself who the man standing in front of her really was. Because if she didn't do that then she was terribly afraid she would agree to this crazy suggestion there and then. But Thorncroft's resident Lothario wasn't really the marrying kind.

'And what of your playboy ways?'

'That part of my life is over.'

'You can simply give that up?' She frowned, as if a part of her didn't feel so joyous at the idea. 'Not just like that.'

'I'm sure I've already told you that those stories were exaggerated anyway.'

'But not complete lies,' she pointed out. 'And even if there's only a fraction of truth in them, how could I expect you to stop completely just because you're married? Especially when ours won't even be a true marriage.'

A sickening thought struck Naomi. So hard that it actually winded her.

'Or are you expecting me to turn a blind eye? Because I can tell you now, that won't happen.'

'I think I rather like the fierce side of you, *älskling*.'

He actually sounded amused, and she had to bite the inside of her mouth to refrain from saying something uncouth.

'But you can sheath your claws, there will be no other women.'

'So you intend to become a monk?' She laughed, though it sounded vaguely maniacal. 'Forgive me if I can't picture it.'

'Who said anything about becoming a monk?' he demanded, his voice low and rich and deep.

And then he was inches from her and suddenly she wasn't laughing any more. Though she was still gasping for air.

Before she knew what she was doing, she found that she'd lifted her hands and splayed them against his chest. It wasn't at all what she'd intended—she had meant to brace against him. But now everything was ten times worse.

A hundred times worse.

Because she was touching him. And the heat of his body was permeating through her hands, and it was all she could do not to give into the crushing urge to let her palms roam the solid chest that felt so deliciously familiar to her.

'I'm not sleeping with you again,' she managed, but her voice was breathy, and unsubstantial.

Was it any wonder? It had been hard enough to get enough air before but now she couldn't breathe at all, which left her feeling light-headed. The *only* reason she was feeling light-headed, she tried telling herself firmly. Because, of course, it couldn't be anything else.

She couldn't possibly be so foolish as to actually believe this ludicrous marriage idea had any legs at all, could she? Worse, she—the girl who had grown up knowing romance and real life bore no relation to each other—couldn't possibly *want* to believe it had any merit.

'Sex,' he corrected thickly. 'Not *sleep.*'

His low, rich tone snaked inside her, winding its way around her chest. Lower and gloriously lower.

Naomi swallowed.

'You can't think I'll have…sex with you again.'

'Oh, I know it,' he rasped. 'Lots of sex. Raw, urgent, desperate sex. As a married couple, we'll have a lifetime of sex together.'

'I don't want that,' she lied, barely recognising her own voice.

His mouth twisted into a smile. He could read the truth in every line of her traitorous body, and there was nothing she could do about it.

'I don't believe that,' he muttered. 'And you don't either.'

And, God, what was wrong with her that he made her ache for him all the more?

It was just the physical, Naomi decided desperately, a physiological reaction. Because that was easier to deal with right now. She had a ready-made excuse for that. And she was dreadfully afraid that if she hadn't had the excuse, she would have willingly given herself to him already.

'Bas... I...'

'Not now,' he assured her. 'Nothing will risk our baby. The next few months will be about doing everything in our power to ensure our unborn daughter gets to term. And we will give our child the stable, family home that neither of us ever got to enjoy.'

It was insane, how badly she wanted to believe him. Standing here with him, like this, she almost did. Naomi had no idea how she found the strength to pull her hands back and step away.

'Real life doesn't work that way,' she managed. 'Couples staying together for the sake of a baby are doomed to fail, never mind one-night stands like us.'

'Personal experience?' He quirked his eyebrow at the emphasis in her tone.

She hadn't meant to say anything. She hadn't even been aware she was going to, until the words came tumbling out of their own volition.

'My mother begged my father to stay, and for a while, he did. I don't have many memories of the time before I lived with my grandmother, but I do remember that it wasn't pleasant living with the constant rowing. Or the screaming and crying.

One often resents the other, or they end up resenting each other. Or they cheat.'

'We will not be *most* couples,' he growled, though he didn't move to close the gap between them again.

'You can't promise that,' she countered softly.

But Bas wasn't so easily deterred.

'I can tell you that I didn't get to be a surgeon by being *most* men, and I didn't get to become a top surgeon by being *most* surgeons.'

From anyone else, it might have sounded arrogant, yet from this man it just sounded factual. Still, it was all she could do not to step back into the circle of his arms, where it had felt safe, yet dangerously thrilling, all at the same time.

'And you didn't get to join the army to look after your family by being *most* women.'

She jerked her head up, the unexpected compliment piercing what little armour she'd been trying to gather about herself.

'Most people are stronger and more resilient than they would give themselves credit for.'

'They are,' he agreed. 'I see it every day, with the way some families rally themselves when a loved one is suddenly desperately ill. Therefore, I see no reason why we can't equally rally together. For this baby.'

'Not if it means me being embarrassed when you finally realise that you can't give up your playboy lifestyle. And I can't quite see you settling down, wife, children, pipe, slippers.'

'No.' He let out an unexpected laugh at that, free and wild, the way she'd only ever seen him be with Grace before that moment. But *she* was the one who had elicited it from him.

It was a heady realisation, as if something were reaching inside her chest, filling it with something she couldn't identify.

Or didn't want to.

How was it that a simple laugh had shifted things between them in an instant?

She didn't realise he'd closed the gap between them until he was there again. And he was dragging a thumb pad across her lower lip.

'But who says our marriage has to be like that?' he demanded. 'We've already demonstrated that we can enjoy a far more…*carnal* connection.'

There was no stopping the delicious shiver that rippled through her at that. Tangling inside her and threatening to turn her inside out. Just from his thumb on her lip.

How quickly would her already weak defence crumble if he replaced his thumb with his mouth?

'I can still taste you,' Bas growled, and she wondered if her thoughts were imprinted, shamefully, on her face somehow. 'In my dreams at night. Some couples make it work on far less.'

Never mind a kiss, how fast would she come apart if he placed his mouth somewhere else altogether? Naomi gasped quietly as the memories came back to her in a rush, charging her right through.

Now, all she could picture was his dark head as it had been nestled between her legs, all those months ago. That expression of wanton greed that had darkened his expression as he'd looked up at her, moments before she'd lost herself completely.

When had any other man affected her quite that way?

It had only ever been Bas.

And then, as if to prove who was in control, he slid his hand around the nape of heck, lowered his head, and claimed her mouth with his own—his skill as devastating as ever. With any other man, it might have been just a kiss. But with Bas, there was no *just* anything.

It was a magnificent assault on her senses. His touch, his smell, his taste, even the way he sounded when he made that low growl of possession that rumbled straight through her. To where she was hottest for him.

Molten.

And even though her brain screamed at her to resist him, to stand firm and demand more from him, to show him that she wouldn't simply capitulate every time, to her shame Naomi felt helpless to stop herself from opening up to his kiss, her body already on fire.

He claimed her again, and again, with the same

wild intensity that she remembered from that first night. Skilful, and bold. Making her his.

And there was nothing she could do about it. She was lost, and she didn't care.

Without warning, Bas stopped. Pulling his head away as he set her body aside from him. Leaving her blinking, and desperately struggling to right herself.

'I rather think that proves the point,' he rasped, his eyes big and black, mirroring her own desire. 'Does it not?'

Naomi didn't answer. She wasn't even sure how she was breathing. Or standing. But one of them needed to walk away from this, otherwise who knew where this night could end up?

Still, she didn't move. In the end, it was Bas who moved across the room. Bas who controlled the shots—as ever.

Because, when it came down to it, she was his— whether she liked it or not. But Bas Jansen wasn't hers in return.

He never would be.

'Talk to me,' Bas instructed as he joined the rest of the multidisciplinary team that had been gathered for the latest case on the resus floor. He'd been finishing a protracted surgery, which had been yet another much-needed distraction from thoughts of Naomi.

He'd been working at the hospital for the last few

days, ever since the night he'd asked her to marry him. Or, more accurately, ever since the kiss when he'd almost forgotten himself completely—the way that only Naomi seemed to make him do.

And though he knew he couldn't avoid her for ever, throwing himself into work seemed like a good temporary option.

'What's the case?' he prompted, biting back his irritation when the doctor didn't answer.

'I'm not running this shout.' The young man edged away, flustered.

Bas blew out a breath.

'Then who is?'

'I am.'

Naomi's unmistakeable voice came over his shoulder, steady and controlled. But even so, it had the ability to reach inside his chest and squeeze. Not that she even gave him a second glance.

'Thirty-two-year-old female came in with significant thermal injuries a short while ago after being caught in a caravan explosion while on holiday with her family,' Naomi advised the team smoothly. Professionally.

Had he expected anything less?

'The patient came to us alert,' Naomi continued, 'though we understand she was unconscious for about a minute on scene. She was intubated for airway protection, and she presented with bilateral breath sounds, and readily apparent full-thickness burns to her face, neck, anterior torso, and bilateral arms, and right leg.'

'Wait.' Stepping forward, Bas made a quick visual check of the patient. This might be Naomi running the shout, but he wasn't about to go easy on her just because working with her was the last thing he needed right now.

So much for his distraction.

Nonetheless, he diverted all his attention to the patient. The extent of her burns was clear enough to see, covering around sixty per cent of her body. 'Secondary imaging?'

'Carried out,' Naomi confirmed. 'No further injuries were revealed. No internal haemorrhaging. I'm bringing her up to the Jansen suite now for excisional debridement of her wounds.'

'Good.' Bas nodded. 'We need to get her into operating room two—the sooner we start, the better for her. Okay, are we ready to move her?'

'Ready.'

'You've taken into account burn shock?'

Naomi nodded.

'Yes, given that it's a major burn covering more than twenty per cent of total body surface injury.'

'Good,' Bas agreed.

The burn shock was a unique combination of distributive and hypovolaemic shock, similar to an ischemia-reperfusion injury manifesting at both cellular, then systemic levels. Early resuscitation of the burns injuries had been proven vital to the survival of a burns victim suffering with burn shock.

'What's your full course of action?'

'I want to get her to the OR for debridement and antimicrobial dressings. She can then resuscitate for the next thirty-six to forty-eight hours with various fluid replacement, bearing in mind the released cytokines with this heat injury, given that the burns are greater than twenty per cent of her total body surface area.'

'Good.' Bas nodded his approval.

Regardless of anything, given the extent of the woman's burns, she would require multiple excisional debridement and wound prep procedures over the course of several weeks, and significant treatment, most likely including cultured epidermal grafts over the coming months, along with local grafts.

'One more thing.' Naomi held Bas back as the porters took over manoeuvring the trolley into the lifts. 'She keeps asking about her son and her husband, but they died in the fire. I don't know whether I'm supposed to tell her or not.'

The twist inside Bas was sharp, and deep.

Just looking at Naomi and thinking about her and their unborn baby suddenly choked him. He didn't even care to imagine how horrific it would be if anything happened to them.

'Do not tell the patient yet,' Bas gritted out under

his breath, though he hated having to keep news like that from somebody.

And the sharp intake of breath from Naomi told him that she felt the same.

'Nothing?'

'Nothing,' he insisted. 'We'll need to keep it from our patient for as long as it takes to get her stable because I can't say what effect that will have on her recovery. And she has enough of a mountain to climb without the added mental anguish.'

As long as the woman was fighting for her life right alongside his medical team, then maybe he could save her life. Though whether she would actually thank him for it was a different thing altogether.

And it struck Bas that if he didn't handle things properly, there was a possibility—in years to come—that neither Naomi nor his unborn baby would thank him for his intervention in their lives, either.

It was late into the night when Naomi and Bas finally finished and were headed back to the penthouse together. In silence. Neither apparently having anything to say.

But that didn't mean her mind wasn't racing. Still trying to process that last, dreadful case.

If working with that young woman had taught Naomi anything, then she thought it had reminded her how short life was.

One moment, her patient had been loving her life with her husband and child. Now, she in the ICU, fighting for her life, and to get back to her family. Not even aware that she didn't have a family to get back to.

Naomi swallowed down the lump that currently clogged up her throat. What if that were her? With Bas, and their daughter?

It didn't bear thinking about.

Shoving the thoughts out of her mind, Naomi hurried to her suite and stripped off her clothes, as though that could somehow help her to also divest herself of the horror of the day. Then, padding through to her en-suite bathroom, she spun the jets for a long, hot shower, and stood under them until her skin was red, and scoured clean.

She couldn't have said how long she stayed like that, but by the time she wandered back through the apartment to find Bas, he was knocking seven shades out of a punchbag in his home gym.

For a short time, she simply stood silently by the door and watched him.

He moved so gracefully that it was almost like a dance. Moving in and out, to one side then the other, as he jabbed and lunged at the heavy bag hanging from the ceiling. It was almost mesmerising.

By the look of the sweat dripping from him, and the pumped muscles, he'd been here a while—probably ever since she'd stepped into the shower—but he showed no sign of stopping.

Was this his way of trying to clear his mind of that dreadful case?

After the other night, she didn't want to step in and invade his space. But neither could she manage to tear herself away. And then, without warning, he turned as though he could sense her there, and Naomi found herself pinned to the spot where she stood.

She thought she ought to speak, but she didn't know what to say. And Bas turned back to the punchbag. *Left-right-left. Right-left-right.*

'That was a bad day,' she blurted out, when she couldn't take it any longer.

Left-right-left.

'We didn't lose our patient.' The exertion made his breath choppy. But she knew that wasn't why it sounded so harsh. 'In fact, we saved her.'

'For what, though?' she whispered. 'When she finds out the truth, she's going to wish we'd let her die right alongside her husband and child.'

Right-left-right.

'For a while.' He shrugged. 'But then…she won't. She'll stop wishing she was dead though she may not like being alive. And then, in time, she'll start living again. It's human nature. Either that, or…'

He stopped talking, but Naomi could hear the words as surely as if he'd spoken them.

And then, the only sound was back to the beating of the punchbag.

'I'm sorry,' she offered eventually. 'I shouldn't have intruded on you.'

Turning, she headed for the door and was halfway through it when Bas stopped and caught the bag.

'Why are you here, Naomi?'

He didn't want to hear what she'd come here to say. But that was too bad, because she needed to tell him. There was nothing else for it.

'What happened today…it made me think.'

'Is that so?' he growled, his voice low.

'Yes.' She forced herself to continue. 'It made me realise that life is too short. You don't know what's around the corner.'

Bas didn't look impressed.

'I've no doubt that working as an army nurse gave you plenty of those days.'

'Not like this.' Naomi took a step forward before she realised what she was doing. 'Today was different.'

And maybe it was because of the baby. Maybe she realised her own mortality. Either way, it didn't change how she now felt. Or how she now *knew* she felt.

'What is it you've come to say, Naomi?' Bas gritted out, his tone far from encouraging.

But she didn't care about that either. She sucked in a steadying breath.

'Today, I realised what I want. What matters to me,' she told him boldly. 'Today, I realised that a marriage in name only isn't what I want.'

Bas dropped the punchbag and took a step towards her. She wondered what made her notice the slight hesitation in his step, as though he wasn't as brimming with confidence as he liked to make out. Or why the bandages on one of his fists were hanging low, as if a part of him was somehow defeated.

As if she was finally seeing the truth behind that suit of armour that he'd always drawn around himself.

'I warned you not to try to take my daughter from me, Naomi,' he bit out.

But she wasn't fooled.

'I'm not trying to take anyone away from you.' She lifted her hands in placation. 'I'm saying that I agree. I'm in.'

'You're in?' He eyed her sceptically.

She told herself there was nothing to feel nervous about.

'Our baby will be better off with both of us in her life. So… I accept.'

'You accept.'

'I do.' Naomi dipped her head, albeit a little jerkily—though she told herself that was nerves, nothing more. 'I will marry you.'

CHAPTER ELEVEN

'PLEASE, YOU HAVE to help me!'

The desperate voice had Naomi jerking her head up from the nurses' station. A young woman gripped the desk white-knuckle tight, her words tumbling urgently out of her mouth.

'I'm looking for my husband. I had a call to say he'd been in an accident this morning. He was hit by a car on his way to work. Oh…he was cycling.'

Quietly, soothingly, Naomi moved to the computer, almost forgetting to reach over her bump—still small for over thirty weeks, but evident nonetheless—as she placed her fingers on the keyboard.

How was she already this far along? It seemed as though the past few weeks…no, wait…*months,* had passed by so quickly with Bas.

Shaking the thought from her head, Naomi focussed on the young woman.

'What is your husband's name?'

'Dave. Dave Kiffleson.'

Naomi paused, not needing to type. She'd been working on that case with Bas a couple of hours ago, when the patient had arrived in Resus—cyclist versus car. A young newly-wed who was little more than a kid.

And now his life was in Bas's hands on the operating table—not that she was about to tell their patient's young, terrified, new wife.

Naomi offered another comforting smile.

'Let me see if I can find someone who can talk to you.'

'Oh, no!' A loud sob escaped the girl's throat as her hands flew up to her mouth. 'It's bad, isn't it? Oh, please don't say he's... I can't be without him. I can't.'

'It's Becky, isn't it?'

Another gasp, as the young woman nodded.

'You spoke to him?'

'A little. Dave was quite badly injured, but he kept wanting us to wait for you to arrive. He said you'd be here any minute.'

'He did?'

The relief was evident.

'He did.' Naomi smiled kindly. There was no need, at this point, to frighten her by telling her that her husband had been slipping in and out of consciousness. Or quite how bad a state his body had been in. 'You're newly-weds, aren't you?'

'Two weeks.' Becky pulled a face that was both awkward and defiant. 'We eloped. Our families said we were too young, but we love each other.'

Naomi didn't react. She had no intention of judging. A part of her even half admired the passion in the girl's voice. The same passion that had been in the young lad's reaction, despite his obvious pain.

What must it be like to love a person that much? To feel as though you couldn't go on if they were no longer in your life? To feel such pure love?

Like the love you're starting to feel for Bas?

The question slammed into her brain from apparently nowhere, and Naomi fought to shove it aside.

The girl peered at her through her tears.

'Oh, you understand exactly what I mean, don't you?' Becky managed to sob out.

'No... I—' Naomi began to speak, but the girl clearly wasn't listening.

'I can see it in your face. You know what I'm saying.'

And as hard as she tried to deny it—if only to herself—Naomi found she couldn't say a word.

She loved Bas.

How had that even happened?

It had snuck up on her so sneakily she hadn't even realised it—ever since that night in his gym when she'd agreed to marry him.

It had been like flicking a switch. As though the assurance that she wasn't trying to tear his daughter away from him had revealed a whole different Bas, who Naomi had never anticipated.

A kind Bas. An attentive Bas. A caring Bas. All revealed in every tiny little thing that he did to make her pregnancy—her life—easier. Each one of them seemingly unimportant in and of themselves yet which, when put together, meant that her life had changed without her even realising it. And for the better.

When had she started to feel as though she mattered—really mattered—to someone? To *Bas*?

When had this...*thing* inside her suddenly flickered into life? When had it breathed out its first body-warming breath, heating up her frozen heart with each passing day?

How had Bas made her feel alive again?

And one day had bled into another, and then into a week, and suddenly she was here, unable to imagine how she would feel if she were Becky, and Bas were Dave. It would be...unbearable. And not simply because he was her unborn daughter's father.

He *mattered* to her. How had that happened?

Thrusting the unwelcome, unhelpful thought from her brain, Naomi turned her full concentration to Becky.

'But we wanted to help him as quickly as we could so your husband is in Theatre right now,' Naomi said firmly but with as much comfort as she could. 'He's with the best people to help him. Let me get someone who can explain what's happening more fully.'

Beckoning a colleague to make the call, Naomi moved around the desk and led the woman to a relatives' waiting area.

'As soon as one of my colleagues comes down, I'll take you through to them.'

'You can't tell me?' Becky pushed anxiously, and Naomi shook her head.

'I'm sorry, but it's better that you speak to one of my colleagues who has been in the OR with your

husband. He'll have far more up-to-date information for you. Can I get you tea? Coffee?'

The girl offered her a momentarily blank look,
then managed a small smile.

'Tea, please.'

'Tea it is.' Naomi dipped her head as she headed
over to the machines.

It felt like the least she could do. Because even if
Bas could save his patient from being wheelchair-
bound for the remainder of his life, the young lad's
spinal injuries meant that it was going to be a long,
long road back to recovery. It would take months
to learn to walk again. Perhaps even years to run
or cycle.

'In sickness and in health,' Becky blurted out as
she returned with the tea.

Naomi caught herself abruptly. Had she uncharacteristically betrayed herself in her expressions?

'Sorry?'

'I was in and out of hospitals as a kid.' The girl
shrugged, suddenly more composed. 'Childhood
leukaemia. I learned to read micro expressions,
though you hide yours pretty well. But I can tell
it's bad.'

'My colleague is the best surgeon I know,' Naomi
offered sincerely as the girl flashed another half-
smile.

'We vowed to love each other in sickness and in
health, and I intend to honour it, whatever happens,'
Becky said firmly. 'I guess I never expected the

sickness to come so soon, and we always thought it would be the cancer coming back for me rather than something happening to him, but it doesn't change anything.'

Naomi choked back an unexpected sob. Put like that, it cast a whole different perspective on how young these two newly-weds were.

'People say *life's too short* all the time,' Becky continued quietly, taking a small sup of her tea. 'But I don't think many of them understand it the way that Dave and I do. And I guess, in this job, you must see that too, right?'

And for a moment, Naomi could only stare at Becky. A wise old woman in the body of a teenager.

'Right,' Naomi managed abruptly. 'Life's too short.'

So what was she going to do about it?

Bas eyed Naomi sceptically. It wasn't so much that he didn't understand the words she was saying, it was more that he didn't understand his body's re-action to them.

Or perhaps he did understand, all too well, and it was more that he feared it.

These last few months with her living in his penthouse had been…a revelation. It had made him see things, feel things, *want* things that he'd never wanted before. And he found the prospect terrifying.

He'd decided over a month ago that it was better

to pretend it didn't exist than have to deal with it. But now, he couldn't ignore it any more. Not when Naomi was standing right in front of him saying all the things he'd never imagined wanting to ever hear anyone say.

He still didn't want to hear, Bas reminded himself brusquely.

'I'm saying that I want more,' she continued defiantly when it became clear he hadn't been intending to answer her.

'More?'

One simple syllable that was a sentence—a warning—all on its own. But Naomi clearly had no intention of heeding it.

'More,' she confirmed. 'More than just a paper marriage. More than just a marriage of convenience. More than just marrying for the sake of our daughter.'

It took him an eternity to answer. And when he did, he wasn't even sure what he was saying.

'More, how?' he managed.

Naomi flicked her tongue out over her suddenly parched lips, but he couldn't help his gaze from being snagged by the motion. His body reacted predictably, even as he tried to shut it down. Having her live with him the past few months, getting closer, had been difficult enough without this added fire in the mix.

'I want something real, Bas. I want love.'

He laughed. An unpleasant sound that scraped, painful and deep, inside his own body.

'*Love?* Love doesn't exist, Naomi. It isn't real. It's an illusory construct dreamt up by those too desperate, too lonely, too pathetic to know better.'

She shook her head.

'It's real, Bas. You want to know how I know?'

'Not really,' he snapped.

She chose to ignore him.

'I know it's real because I feel it. For you.'

'No.'

'I love you, Bas.'

The silence between them was oppressive. Menacing even. Though he didn't know if it was only him who felt it.

Something boiled through Bas and even though that terrified part of him feared it wasn't temper— not at all—a dull part of his brain channelled it into such. Because it was easier to be angry than to face whatever that dark, viscous...*thing* was that swirled within him.

'You do not love me.'

Still, he didn't realise he'd roared the denial until it began bouncing back to him, off the cold, stark walls.

He wanted to punch it away again. Keep it from touching him. But at the same time, there was a deep ache in his chest. A yearning, that began to cleave him in two right there, where he stood. And there was no punching *that* away.

'People do not love me, Naomi,' he tried again, even though he barely recognised his own voice.

'And yet I do.' She offered a smile so soft that he thought it might suffocate him. 'There is nothing fundamentally unlovable about you, at all. I love you. Grace does, in a different way. That much is evident. Even Henrik, I think. Since he came all this way.'

'That's impossible,' he made himself insist. Though he couldn't explain why it was getting harder and harder to remember a truth he'd known all these years. 'Henrik isn't capable of it, any more than I am.'

'You're wrong.' She flashed that damned soft smile again. 'I think you're capable of a lot more than you like to pretend.'

'No.'

'You didn't take me—us—in because it was your duty, or at least you didn't take us in *simply* because you felt it was your duty. You took us in because I am carrying your daughter.'

'Why do you seem so intent on thinking of me as a much better man than I actually am?'

'Why do you seem so intent on seeing yourself as less than you are?'

And Bas thought it was that gentleness that might prove his undoing. He wanted to refute what she was saying. He found he couldn't. He wasn't sure what that said about the situation.

'I'm taking responsibility for my child. That is a matter of doing what is right. That isn't about love.'

'Except that we don't need to get married in order for you to meet your responsibilities.'

'This baby will have two parents who care for her. To…'

'To love her?' Naomi supplied when he stopped. 'When I told you I was pregnant, I did so because I knew it was morally the right thing to do. But I told you, even then, that I didn't want or expect anything from you.'

'So because I chose to take my responsibility seriously, you think that means I love you?' he demanded. 'I have no wish to hurt you, Naomi, but that wasn't love. I told you, I'm not capable of such an emotion. I wish I were.'

'You *are* capable, Bas.' Naomi shook her head. 'I think you only wish you *weren't*. Which makes me wonder if talking to Henrik is the solution. Not so long ago I asked you if you couldn't forgive Henrik because what happened when you were kids is still too painful for you, or if it was more that it has been so long that you no longer know *how* to forgive him.'

'I didn't answer you,' he bit out.

'You did not,' she agreed. 'And now I know why. Because it's both of those things. And it's something else as well.'

'No.'

'Yes,' she continued gently. 'The reason you won't

forgive Henrik—the reason you still hate him—
is because you're scared of yourself, Bas. You're
scared to love again. Him. Me. Our baby. And that's
why you keep everyone at arm's length.'

'You're wrong,' he rasped, wishing that there
weren't that unwelcome sliver of him that thought
it might agree with her.

'Are you sure about that?' She pressed her lips
against each other sadly. 'Because I wonder what
your brother has come all this way to tell you. Why
he turned his back on you for all those years?'

'I don't care.'

If only that were true. It *ought* to be true.

'I think we both know that isn't true,' she told
him, as if reading his mind. 'Why you refuse to
meet him. What you've buried in the recesses of
your memory that you don't want dredged up. Are
you hiding from him? Or yourself?'

Bas stood paralysed. Frozen right through. He
had no idea how he managed to work his jaw
enough to reply, but he barely recognised his own
tight, seething voice.

'He betrayed me, Naomi,' he managed. 'He lied
almost thirty years ago to social services, choosing
our excuse for a mother, and the man who had no
right being any child's stepfather, over me—when
I was the only one standing up for him.

'And it has eaten you up inside ever since,' she
exclaimed. 'Yet right now you have the chance
to find out the truth about why Henrik did that.

Maybe he had a good reason to? At the very least, maybe he wants to apologise.'

'It's too late for apologies.' Bas snorted, not surprised at the earnest expression that crossed Naomi's lovely features.

It might have been endearing, had he not felt so livid. And so...knocked sideways.

'I don't think it's ever too late for that,' she told him softly. 'And I'm not saying that if he did apologise you would have to forgive and forget. I'm just saying, for your own sake, let it give you some peace.

Another wave of silence washed over them as he couldn't help wondering if she had a point.

What was the use of all this bitterness and hatred he felt towards his brother? What good did it do him? But even as the thoughts entered Bas's head, another thought chased them along.

'If he came to Thorncroft to apologise, then he shouldn't have tracked down my closest friend and seduced her. He made her betray you, too.'

'Grace never betrayed you,' Naomi countered. 'She was devastated when she found out who he was, you said it yourself. And what if Henrik really didn't know who she was? What if he simply fell for her that night? No ulterior motives.'

'That's ludicrous,' Bas barked. 'No one—'

'Like the way I fell for you,' she continued, refusing to let him take over. 'Like the way I think you feel for me, too. If only you'd let go long enough to see it for yourself.'

'This is not a conversation we will be having.'

He moved back to the punchbag then, dismissing her. Every fibre of her ached on his behalf. His demons were right there, on the periphery, and she couldn't just let him hide away from them for another thirty years. She wouldn't.

Lurching forward, she grabbed the heavy PVC bag as it hung there, stopping Bas from continuing.

'You need to let go,' Naomi whispered. 'You've been clinging to the edge for so long without knowing it.'

'This isn't going to happen. It's in the past. I'm not going to speak to Henrik. He may be a good surgeon but he is my brother in name only. I have no intention of meeting with him.'

'I can't help feeling that would be your loss, Bas,' she pleaded.

His face twisted into a mask of ferocious hurt, though she doubted he realised it.

'So be it.'

'Let go. And if you fall, I'll be here to catch you.'

'I will not fall,' he growled. 'And, if I did, I would never need you to catch *anything*.'

He hadn't wanted to hurt her, but he'd needed to stop her from talking. He'd needed to do something—anything—to stop the sharpness of her words from stabbing into him like a thousand tiny needle points.

Even so, he wasn't ready for the look of anguish that twisted up her lovely face.

'Then if you can't let go of those awful parts of your past,' she choked out, 'you need to let go of me.'

'Say again?'

'I love you, Bas. But that means that I can't watch you devouring yourself from the inside out. I don't want to see you putting yourself through that suffering over and over, like it's on some kind of crazy loop in your head.'

'What exactly are you saying?' Bas bit out coldly, as Naomi threw her arms around herself as if to ward off anything bad.

'I'm saying that you should let me go, Bas. Forget marriage. Or living together to raise this child. You're Basilius Jansen, of course. Thorncroft's resident playboy surgeon. I knew you would remember that eventually, however much we both tried to pretend otherwise.'

'You tried to pretend otherwise,' he ground out, hating himself. 'I seem to recall warning you who I was all along.'

'Someone who is incapable of love. Or forgiveness. Or even basic human decency. Yes, you're making that as clear as you can, aren't you, Bas? Well, then, fine. Have it your way. But you need to let me go back to my grandmother and my sister.'

'I think not.'

'I think yes,' she countered. 'I need to go home. More than that, my baby needs to come with me. She deserves better than you, Bas. She deserves a family. People who won't be afraid to tell her that they love her. Who will teach her how to be a better person.'

And if Naomi had taken a scalpel to his chest, and sliced it wide open, it surely couldn't have pained him any more than this.

For several moments, he couldn't answer. He was sure he stopped breathing.

'Fine,' he heard himself answer, at long last. 'That might indeed be for the best.'

And if she looked destroyed, then there was very little he could do about that. He felt decimated.

It was sickening to realise that this baby—his unborn daughter—would be better off without him.

That he wasn't the kind of role model she should ever have to deal with in her life.

'No marriage. No contact between you and I,' he continued. 'But that is still my daughter, and I won't let her be taken from my life so easily.'

'I'll move back home, until I…we…come to some kind of arrangement.'

'As you wish,' he agreed coldly, ignoring the tumbling and twisting inside him at that moment. 'I'll sort out a more appropriate apartment for you—one that is closer to the hospital, but where you can live with your family without being on top of each other.'

'I don't need you to take care of me. I need you to—'

He cut her off again.

'It's done, Naomi.'

If only his mind were as clear as his voice sounded. What else did he need to sort out? His thoughts were a confusion of emotions.

She had just had her last weekly foetal nonstress test; it would be another week before there was another.

Bas vacillated. The tests checked for movements because she couldn't feel much any more, beyond the usual pain from sheer fluid. But the baby had been fine the past few weeks, and he didn't care to deal with Grace at the moment. Most importantly, he didn't want any confrontation between the two of them to upset Naomi.

For her sake, it would be better for him not to be there this time.

If he could have wrapped her, and his baby, in cotton wool and tucked them away in his apartment, not to emerge for the remainder of the pregnancy, then he was sure he would have done so. And the notion bewildered him.

He, who had never wanted children. Or a family. Or even a wife. He, who had never felt so protective of any woman who he'd dated. Although, admittedly, *dated* probably wasn't the most appropriate term.

Which brought him to the other reason behind hauling the mother of his unborn baby to his private apartment.

Had a part of him hoped that bringing her here, to his 'sanctuary' where he'd never brought a lover in all his life, might help him to get a grip on whatever this *thing* was between them?

As unchivalrous as it was, Bas considered that such a motive had indeed formed part of his plan. But then, how chivalrous could a self-proclaimed playboy really be?

He suspected that he'd imagined seeing her here would feel wrong. Ill-fitting. And might thus help to dull this inconvenient attraction he felt for her.

But it hadn't helped at all.

It was still there, squatting on his chest. A little too bright, and too encompassing.

CHAPTER TWELVE

BAS POUNDED THE STREETS, running faster, harder, better than he'd ever done in his life.

But he didn't feel better.

He felt as if he were a mere shadow of himself. The last month without Naomi had been torture. His own private hell, which more and more he was beginning to think he'd brought upon himself.

He was free. Back to his pre-Naomi, pre-baby life. His apartment was his own. His lawyers were drawing up the contracts for Naomi to sign.

Finally, he could begin to breathe again.

Only, he couldn't seem to.

Instead, every last second of their row began to run through his head. Replaying in all too vivid detail. To his shame.

The way she'd looked. And that devastated expression on her lovely features when he'd sliced her with his words. As if she truly believed what she'd been telling him. As if she truly couldn't see the darkness that lurked within that made him so impossible to love. Or, that he'd always believed made him impossible to love.

And if he was, in fact, deserving of the love of a woman like Naomi, then could she also be right that he was capable of love, too?

He picked up his speed to a brutal pace, but it didn't help.

Everything swelled and crashed through Bas's brain, shifting and tilting the way his whole life seemed to have been doing recently. Starting with the night he'd met Naomi and peaking the night he'd severed her from his life.

He could still picture the way she'd looked. The way she'd felt in his arms as they'd swept across that floor together. She hadn't known how to dance, and still, the way she had followed his lead as though they were one and same. Handcrafted for each other.

And nothing dulled the pain.

Once upon a time, whiskey had numbed his feelings. Peaty and rich, it had seemed to help him to fool himself that life was good. But now he found he could barely touch it. Naomi had changed everything. Taking him higher than he'd ever felt before. More intoxicated than ever, without ever having had a drop.

He just hadn't wanted to admit it.

Suddenly, he realised that he didn't want to argue any more. At least, not with her. Not with the woman who had brought him back to life when he hadn't even realised that he'd been dead inside.

As much as he loathed the idea of speaking with Henrik—good surgeon or not—he could concede that Naomi had made a good point when she'd reminded him that they were all different people than they had been ten, twenty, thirty years ago.

So, even if he knew his brother could have nothing to say that Bas wanted to hear, he could at least hear Henrik out. If only for Naomi. And if only for the baby that was growing in her belly.

He was soon to be a father, with all that entailed. The least he could do was be one worthy of their daughter.

Turning back to the house, Bas began running faster, despite the fact that his legs no longer felt as if they were his.

Home.

Or at least, he would be, once he brought Naomi back. And soon—their daughter.

'What the hell happened?'

Bas burst into the hospital, his lungs on fire. He wasn't sure he'd breathed ever since he'd returned to his penthouse only to see a missed message.

Naomi turned her head to him and his stomach twisted at the expression of pure anguish in her eyes.

'What are you doing here, Bas?'

'Your sister left me a message.'

The words felt strange in his mouth, and he realised it was the fact that Leila shouldn't have had to call him in the first place. He should have been there. He should have never let Naomi go through this alone.

But this wasn't the time or the place.

'What happened, Naomi?'

'I don't need you here,' she bit out. The pained expression belying her words.

But it was only what he deserved.

'We can talk about how much of a lie that is later,' he managed. 'Just as we can talk about what a jerk I've been.'

Naomi gritted her teeth.

'You don't want to be here. You said it from the start. It's fine.'

'I was wrong,' he said, shocking her. 'I was coming to tell you that when I got the message.'

'You were?'

She lifted her hands up and stopped. As if she'd been going to reach for him but had thought better of it.

Bas took her hands in his.

'I was,' he assured her. 'But now isn't the time. What happened?'

She looked at him, then exhaled on a shaky breath.

'Grace found an issue during this week's foetal nonstress test. They brought me straight into hospital.'

Bas didn't dare speak. He bit back a curse. This wasn't a scenario with which he was familiar, and still all he could do was try to keep from swaying on precarious legs as he stared at her.

'What was the issue?'

Naomi swallowed once, twice, as she fought not

to cry, and Bas found himself hurrying across the room to take her hands.

Her grip was white-knuckle tight.

'The baby's heart-rate dipped a couple of times so they carried out an ultrasound. I'm having contractions.'

'Contractions?'

His gut twisted further. She was thirty-six weeks; if the baby was born now it would be preterm. Late pre-term, but pre-term all the same.

'I'm in labour, Bas.' There was no mistaking the agony in her voice. It echoed that dark thing that was currently skulking around his chest. 'And I couldn't even feel it.'

'That's not uncommon,' Grace said quietly, returning to the room. 'With all the fluid, and the discomfort you've been feeling up to this point.'

'So bed rest?' Bas cut in, unable to help himself. 'You can give her something to stop the contractions, Grace. Betamimetics? Try to keep the baby in just a little longer. Preferably to at least thirty-seven weeks.'

'Her cervix is already beginning to change and your little one isn't tolerating the contractions too well.' Grace shook her head, before turning back to Naomi. 'We'll prep you for a C-section now, Naomi.'

'I'm coming in.' Bas lifted the side of the bed and prepared to move it.

'You'll wait here,' Grace told him firmly. 'I'll

take good care of her, Bas. But you're the father right now, not the surgeon. I'll make sure we call you as soon as she's prepped.

There was an unspoken test in there, and Bas knew they were both waiting to see whether he trusted his friend enough to look after Naomi. And he didn't care. All that mattered was her. And their baby.

'Go,' he grunted, dipping his head to kiss Naomi's forehead.

Words hovered on his lips, but he couldn't say them. Not yet. Not until he'd done what she'd asked him to do.

He sat in the room for what felt like a lifetime. Maybe two. And even Bas—accustomed to the speed of treatment during a medical emergency—found he wasn't processing it as he might have expected.

It was one thing being the surgeon in control of the event, but quite another being this side of a scenario, at risk of being consumed by his concern for both the baby, and the mother of his unborn child.

And then, finally, a midwife came for him. He wasn't sure how he managed not to run down the corridors to the operating room, barely noticing as they gowned him up and led him through.

The sight of her on the operating table wasn't one he was prepared for. He'd performed countless procedures over the years, but this was surreal. *Unconscionable.*

'The local anaesthetic means you won't feel any pain as we pull the baby out, Naomi, but you'll be aware of the movement.' Grace smiled kindly. 'I've had some patients describe it as being a little like a washing machine churning around.'

'Understood.' Naomi forced a tight smile of her own, even as she reached for his hand again, gripping it just as tightly as before.

Bas didn't dare to look around the curtain. He just kept his eyes locked with Naomi's, talking to her as quietly and soothingly as possible, though he wasn't sure he had any idea what he was talking to her about.

And then, at last, their baby was out and he stopped breathing, his stomach twisted into the tightest knot as they manually cleared her airways and the room was silent, waiting for that first cry.

'Is she okay?' Naomi choked out as the silence seemed to stretch on for an eternity. 'Is she…alive?'

He moved his hand to stroke the hair from her face, not trusting himself to answer. Then, without warning, a loud cry rent the air and Bas thought it was possibly the most beautiful sound that he'd ever heard.

'She's strong.' Grace appeared, the tiny bundle in her arms. 'Do you want to hold her before we take her through to NICU?'

Naomi lifted her arms and took her daughter, staring in awe at the tiny, puckered face. If he could have frozen this moment for ever, he thought he might have. And then Naomi glanced up at him and carefully offered their daughter for him to take.

'I've carried her for eight months,' she whispered. 'I think it's your chance now.'

He didn't wait to be told again. Taking his new baby in his arms, Bas looked down in undiluted rapture.

She was more perfect than he could have imagined. And he couldn't even speak to tell Naomi. He didn't need to. Once glance at her face told him she knew it too.

Holding their baby out for Naomi to kiss, he touched his own lips to her head.

'Aneka,' Naomi whispered reverently. Like a prayer.

'Aneka,' Bas echoed quietly. Then, long before he was ready, Grace appeared to reluctantly take her away again.

'Sorry,' she murmured, extending her arms.

Bas couldn't answer. His whole world had up-ended in an instant, and it hadn't even taken him a full glance to realise there was nothing he wouldn't do for this baby.

This was love—*real* love. And he was capable of it.

More than capable. It felt as though he had been waiting for this moment—for these two incredible human beings to enter his life. This wasn't about being a husband and father because it was the right thing to do, this was about being a husband and father because he knew his life would be all wrong if he didn't.

He loved them. And that meant he wanted to be the best version of himself that he could possibly be.

There was one thing left to do.

'Thank you,' he murmured sincerely as Grace turned to look at him.

Her smile broadened.

'Any time.'

Beside him, Naomi squeezed his hand once again, though she didn't say anything.

She didn't need to.

Bas watched as they took the baby to the NICU, then he waited for them to take Naomi to post-op recovery. And then he peeled off his gown and left the OR.

His new life with Naomi, and their daughter, could start the moment he spoke to Henrik. It might be the closure that Naomi had once suggested he needed.

Or maybe, just maybe, it could end up being so much more than that.

'I was surprised to receive your call.'

A few weeks ago it would have taken every ounce of Bas's self-control to look at his brother without reacting. As though his presence didn't both Bas at all.

Now, here in the hospital coffee shop, he couldn't

help but notice that he didn't feel the same antagonism. Naomi——and now their beautiful little Aneka——were having more of an effect on him than he could ever have imagined possible. Healing him; making him feel whole for the first time in his life.

'Let's get on with this, shall we?' he suggested instead.

'How is fatherhood?' Henrik asked without warning.

'Fine,' began Bas. But it was impossible not to say more when his chest felt as if it might swell enough to burst. 'I never thought I would ever be a parent, yet I've learned how to be a father. A proper father. I've begun to understand what it is to love, and to accept love.'

'And you didn't know that before?'

The tone of the questions was like a grate rubbing the wrong way over Bas's soul.

'How could I know?' he demanded. 'I had no idea what love felt like. It's taken me until now to understand it.'

'Then I envy you.' Henrik bowed his head slightly, leaving Bas confused.

'You envy me? Are you completely deluded?'

'I always envied you. You got away.'

'I got away? I was the one who envied you.'

Henrik looked genuinely confused.

'I can't imagine why.'

'You had it all,' Bas blasted out. 'You were the

one she wanted—the one she heaped love onto—whilst I was the one she cast aside.'

'Say that again,' Henrik demanded slowly, his tone unexpectedly dangerous.

Not that Bas was remotely cowed. Not when his stomach was churning so violently.

'You were the one she wanted to keep, whilst I was the one she couldn't wait to get rid of.'

'Have you seriously forgotten what it was like in that house when things didn't go our stepfather's way? Did you consider that, with you gone, I was the only punchbag left? Did you think she'd suddenly stop turning a blind eye to his tempers?'

'That was your decision. You're the one who told authorities I was lying when I'd had enough. At least she wanted to keep you. I got sent to be with a father who never wanted me around.'

'You can't really mean that?' The chill in Henrik's tone could have frosted the entire hospital.

But Bas didn't care. He gritted his teeth at his brother.

'How do you think it feels to be the son so awful that even his mother couldn't love him? I spent years wondering what was so wrong...so flawed about me, that wasn't you. You were always the perfect son.'

'That's...preposterous.' Henrik shook his head in disbelief, and Bas felt his own temper rise.

Bas took a step back, folding his arms over his

chest—whether to protect himself or to create a barrier from his brother, he couldn't be sure.

'That's the truth. The last words she told me were that you and I might be twins, but that I lacked your compassionate side. That I was a horrid little bastard who no one could ever love.'

'Is that what you truly think?' Henrik laughed, but it was a hollow, cold sound.

Bas stopped, taken aback.

'Is that the way you remember things in your head, Basilius? That she somehow favoured me?'

'Didn't she?'

'No.' Henrik didn't hesitate. 'Our mother was a master of manipulation. She used to tell me that I lacked the kind of personality that you had. She told me that I was a pathetic excuse for a boy, and that no one could ever love me.'

Bas didn't answer. How could he when he had no idea what to say?

'Have you really forgotten what our mother was truly like?' Henrik demanded, after a moment. 'Have you forgotten how she used to play one of us against the other? Always trying to drive that wedge between us? All for attention?'

'I haven't forgotten anything,' Bas ground out. 'I remember how she more than loved attention, she *craved* it. She couldn't live without it. Attention to her was like air is to every other normal human being. Without it, she might as well be suffocating, dying. And you gave it to her.'

'I was trying to keep her sweet.' His brother shook his head. 'In a good mood. Especially when *he* came along, and it went from her manipulation to his fists.'

There was no need to discuss him further, they both knew who they were talking about.

'You never really bore the brunt of that, did you?' Bas couldn't help saying.

He wasn't prepared for his brother's response.

'Not as much as you did, I know that. You made sure of it.'

He paused, as if waiting for Bas to acknowledge, but the memories were hazy, and Bas couldn't work out what he was supposed to be remembering.

'Don't you remember how you would take the blame for me?' Henrik demanded. 'Taking responsibility for things I was supposed to have done wrong, even though you'd had nothing to do with it? If we were out of milk. If a light had been left on. Even simply if we walked down the stairs the wrong way.'

'I remember all that,' Bas began, 'but I don't remember taking the blame for you.'

'Well, you did.' His brother jerked his head. 'Almost all the time. You were always a protector, Basilius. Even for me. The only reason you didn't try to protect me that day was because you were concussed. Not that either of us understood that at the time.'

'Say that again?'

'You got walloped the day before. Only, it was so rough that you'd actually been sick. You told me that everything had gone black. If it hadn't been for that, you would have leaped in for me again. The way you always did.'

Bas stared down his six-foot-three brother. It was anybody's guess which of them might have a millimetre's edge on the other. And the images were fuzzy, but, now that Henrik had reminded him of them, something was beginning to pull into focus.

Henrik had been born half an hour after him, and hadn't he himself always felt like the *big* brother, needing to protect his younger brother?

'So why did you betray me?' Bas demanded abruptly; the one question that had niggled at him most, all these years, finally spilling out. 'Why did you back her up, that final time, instead of me?'

Henrik peered at him, incredulously.

'Because we agreed that was what I was going to do.'

Bas could only gawk at him.

'What are you talking about?' he ground out. 'Why would we ever, *ever* agree that?'

Disbelief was etched into his brother's face.

'You really don't remember?'

He felt as though he were going to explode.

'Remember what?'

'We agreed that if Child Welfare took us, then they'd probably end up splitting us up. We didn't want that.'

'That conversation never happened,' Bas scorned. His memories might be hazy, but they weren't non-existent. 'Besides, we got split up anyway.'

'How could we have foreseen that?' his brother bit out. 'We didn't know Magnus existed. We didn't even know that deadbeat wasn't our father.'

That much was true enough. But as for the rest of it...

'So that's what you're claiming? That was our plan?' He was getting angry now. And he couldn't seem to swallow it down. 'That we agreed I would tell the truth, only for you to back up our mother's lie? I don't think much of that so-called plan.'

'Our plan was that we would get rid of Child Welfare, and then we were going to run away and find Mrs P and Bertie,' Henrik fired back. 'You really don't remember?'

'I don't remember because it didn't happen.'

It was a strong denial. And yet, still, it cleaved into two that hard ball of resentment and anger inside him.

'It must have been the concussion,' Henrik realised abruptly.

And Bas hated that it made sense.

Hated it, and at the same time wished with every fibre of his being that it could be true.

That maybe his brother never had betrayed him the way he'd thought, all those years ago.

'You're saying you told them that I was lying so that they would go away?'

Surely it was sickening how desperate he sounded. Not that Henrik seemed to have noticed. He was wearing his own fervent expression.

'And we wouldn't be torn apart before we'd had chance to escape and find Mrs P,' Henrik added.

The two men stood in contemplative silence.

Could it really be that simple? He wished his memory weren't so hazy. But then what Henrik had said about a concussion would make sense.

The strangest part about it all was that Bas thought he might actually believe his brother. Because he *wanted* to believe Henrik? Or because his subconscious knew something he didn't? He couldn't be sure.

'I tried to find you,' his brother offered, after another pause. 'But I had no idea where to start looking or how. I asked, but she never told me anything, of course.'

'I find that harder to believe. Even back then, Magnus Jansen had made a name for himself as a surgeon.'

Henrik cast him a long look.

'Up until our mother's death, before Christmas last year, I thought my name was Henrik Magnusson. I've spent a decade looking up every Magnusson in Sweden. I had no idea you were even in the UK, let alone that I should really be looking for the name Jansen. The only thing I ever gleaned from her, growing up, was that he was a surgeon. It was the one nugget I held onto. So damned tightly. My one connection to you.'

'So much so that you became a surgeon?' Bas rasped.

It sounded so plausible, but he hated the idea that he might be being gullible.

'Yes.'

So simple. So frank. It rattled Bas—the idea that he might have got it all wrong, all these years.

'You expect me to believe that you only found out the truth when our mother told you...what, on her deathbed?'

'I can't tell you what to believe, Basilius. I can only tell you the facts as I know them to be. And she didn't tell me anything, whether on her death-bed or otherwise. Finally telling the truth would have been too kind an ending for her, Basilius. She was bitter and vengeful until the end.'

'Then how?' Bas bit out.

'When she died, Mrs P saw the obituary in the paper and made contact. When I told her what had happened all those years ago, she was able to fill in some of the gaps. Once I pieced it together with what I knew, I was able to find you.'

Bas felt as though he'd been walloped in the gut. It took him a moment to regroup.

'Mrs P is still out there?'

'She is.'

'And Bertie?'

Henrik's expression changed. 'He died. About a

decade ago. Apparently, they'd both been waiting. Hoping we would one day seek them out.'

'They didn't seek us out,' Bas gritted out, as though he didn't care.

When this swirling mess inside him betrayed just how much he really did.

'They didn't know where we'd gone, Basilius. And they didn't want to risk causing problems for us when we were younger. They'd hoped that with them out of the picture, our mother's jealousy would have dissipated. And when we never got in touch, they let themselves believe it.'

He grunted, unable to speak.

'She would love to know about you and Naomi. I can only imagine how much joy it would bring her to hear about your new baby girl.'

Bas jerked his hand up for Henrik to stop.

It was too much to take in at once—his head was swimming. He needed time to process. Even just a moment to breathe.

Henrik, it seemed, had other ideas.

'You seem to think you have the monopoly on being rejected, *bror*. On being mistreated, and wronged. But, from my perspective, you got the better deal. You got away from her. And maybe Magnus wasn't any more welcoming, or loving, I can't speak to that,' Henrik rasped, 'but at least his fists were never the answer.'

Bas glowered at Henrik as though it was all somehow his brother's fault. The man—the surgeon—standing opposite him wasn't quite the stranger he'd always told himself.

Naomi had told him that, at the very least, he might get some closure. But this felt as far from closure as was possible.

'How long did you stay?'

Henrik's expression was closed off, but he forced himself to speak all the same.

'I got away when I was fifteen. Then, as soon as I could, I joined the army and I got my education that way.'

Clearly, his brother wasn't even telling Bas the half of it. He didn't need to. What little he was saying was enough.

It meant that Henrik was more like Naomi than he himself. Only she'd had her grandmother, and her sister. And he'd had Magnus.

Henrik was right—any of those choices would have been better than their mother. Or, worse, their stepfather.

'What about him?' Bas forced himself to ask. 'Where is he now?'

Henrik scoffed indelicately.

'Who knows? Without you or me there as a punchbag, he turned his attention onto her. She saw her chance to take him to court for compensation and she divorced him.'

Bas stopped breathing.

So she'd been willing to stay with him when he'd hurt Henrik or himself—innocent babies, just like his own precious Aneka, who needed his protection more than anyone—but when it came to him hitting her, everything changed?

It felt as if his life had been smashed wide open, exposing some great, cavernous black hole that he'd spent his entire life trying to fill. Work, whiskey, women. He hadn't cared. He'd tossed it all in there and when it had been swallowed up, he'd slung in some more.

And then Naomi had come along. Her brilliance, and warmth, and...love...were all counter to that void within him.

She'd brought colour into his life for the first time in so, so long. She'd given him Aneka.

Family.

And now, she might even have delivered his brother—and Mrs P—back to him. It was more than he'd ever thought possible. More than he'd dared to dream.

More than he deserved. It was going to take him a lifetime—more—to repay her.

And suddenly, he couldn't wait to start.

CHAPTER THIRTEEN

'WHERE EXACTLY IS it that we're going?' Naomi asked the driver as the car glided silently through the quiet streets. Not quite the direction for Bas's penthouse.

She'd been in the NICU, reading to Aneka, for the past few hours. Her baby was growing stronger and stronger with each passing day, and it seemed that tomorrow was going to be the moment she'd been waiting for. The moment when Grace was going to finally operate on her tiny baby girl.

It made Naomi feel elated, and terrified, all at once.

She was only grateful that she'd been able to lean on Bas. He was the only reason she was ever able to tear herself away from the incubator. Because even though he was never there when she was, she knew he had nurses monitoring her coming and going, and the moment she left through one door, she saw him step through the doors at the other end.

'I'm under instructions just to drive you, ma'am,' Phillip apologised.

Of course he was, Naomi thought irascibly. It was another way for Bas to keep his distance. For him to close himself off. For a moment, in that delivery room, she'd felt as though everything had shifted.

As though she'd finally pierced through that armour of ice, after so many weeks of chipping away where she hadn't even managed to make a dent. Or every time she'd thought she had, something had happened and it had iced over once again. And each time, harder than the last.

But none of that was Phillips's fault, so she simply offered him a soft smile.

'I understand.'

It was alarming quite how quickly she'd come to rely on Bas, Naomi thought as she stared out of the window, but instead found herself staring at her own reflection. She who had always been the one other people relied on.

At least, it *ought* to have been alarming. Instead, she'd found it somewhat thrilling. But from the moment they'd called it quits that night, she'd felt lost. Alone. The past month had been like some kind of hell, though she'd gritted her teeth and smiled through it.

What good could come of worrying Leila and her grandmother by sharing the fears that kept her up night after night?

Such as if her baby was going to be okay. And if she could really do this alone.

But this is what you wanted, she reminded herself sternly.

Far better to be alone and know it, than to be with someone who she loved—but who would never let himself love her in return. A man who left her feeling lonelier than ever. And if he couldn't love her—or their precious daughter—the way they would love him, then it would only be all the more hurtful to them both.

Didn't she know that from experience?

There was nothing worse than loving a parent who could never really love in return.

For a brief, reckless moment, she had considered asking Grace to contact Henrik for her, thinking that perhaps if she better understood what had happened when Bas had been a kid, she might be able to help him—and their daughter.

Now she was grateful that she'd dismissed the crazy idea almost as quickly.

No matter the circumstances, this was still Bas's secret. She couldn't violate it. Not even for Aneka.

But if he loved her the way she suspected he did—even if he hadn't admitted it to himself—then he would work it out for himself.

In the meantime, she could focus all her attention on her beautiful daughter. And trust that whatever was going to be, would be.

It was only as the car turned onto the main drag that Naomi felt a prickle of…anticipation. She wasn't sure why, but she realised she'd been holding her breath. Every one of her limbs felt leaden and when the driver rounded the car to open the door for her, Naomi wasn't convinced that she'd be able to slide out.

She wanted *too much*. And she was terrified of how desperate and hopeful that made her.

And then, without warning, he was there. *Bas*. Opening the door and reaching in to offer his hand.

Wordlessly, she took it, allowing him to draw her out of the limousine, and into his arms. She waited, her entire body yearning for him to simply lower his mouth and kiss her.

But he didn't.

'What's this about, Bas?' Her tongue felt too out-sized for her mouth.

Tucking her hand through his elbow by way of an answer, Bas turned her around to look at the house.

'It isn't the country home with the rambling roses, or the pretty fence. But it is a family house, with a playroom, and a garden. Even a kitchen where you could make jam, if only you didn't burn the water trying to boil an egg.'

She craned her neck to look at him and he offered a soft laugh.

'Oh, you thought I didn't notice? You were with me long enough to reveal a few flaws in your otherwise perfect character.'

'Hardly,' she breathed, but the emotion in his voice was what slid inside her the most.

The warmth.

Turning back, she gazed up at the Georgian town house with the stone steps leading up to the big door. A warm light spilling out of the semicircular window above it.

'It's perfect.'

'It's ours. If you want it,' he told her. 'A family house, but together we can make it a home.'

For Naomi, in that moment, time might as well have stopped. Or perhaps sped up, whirling around on some unseen lever before hurtling off into nothingness.

And it was hard to remember all the reasons why she'd walked away from him, when Bas was gazing at her with such unadulterated love in his eyes.

But she *had* to remember them. Because they hadn't changed.

Had they?

'I should have realised eight months ago that you were the thing I didn't know I'd been looking for, my entire life,' he told her. 'I knew you were different from the first moment we met. When I saw you moving around that room, I thought you'd reached inside and stolen my breath, but now I know you stole something far, far more valuable.'

'I want to believe you,' she whispered. 'I do. But you're talking about half measures. You won't even talk to your brother because you don't believe in love. Or forgiveness.'

'I believe in them now,' he confirmed, with a certain steadiness to his tone that convinced her every bit as much as the words themselves. 'I don't want half measures, either, *älskling*. I thought I was better alone. I thought I was incapable of love. But I was wrong. You unlocked something inside me that I could never have believed existed.'

Naomi wanted to speak; her throat, her chest, ached with the need to say something. But she couldn't. She could only listen, transfixed, as Bas stood in front of her, his hand brushing a stray strand of hair from her face in a movement that was so simple, yet so intimate, that it stole the breath from her lungs.

'I'm a different man with you in my life, a *better* man. And I want our daughter to know that man. I don't want to be my father. I thought I did, but now I realise how much he lost out on. He was the kind of man who held onto things tightly, with his fists. Grasping them so tightly that he ended up suffocating them. All the way, never acknowledging that he needed or wanted them at all.'

Without warning, he dropped to one knee.

'Over the better part of the past three decades, I've learned to silence all my rage, and frustration. But along with that, I learnt to stuff down everything that could make me a better man. That isn't the kind of father, or husband, I want to be. I want to be the best version of myself, and you are the only person who has helped me to find that.'

'Bas…'

Pulling an elegant box out of his pocket, he lifted it up until it was between then, but didn't open it.

'You told me you wanted more, that you *deserved* more. And you were right.

'You made me face up to my demons. More than

that, Naomi, you gave me the weapons I needed to defeat them.'

'Henrik was never your demon,' she choked out.

'No, he wasn't,' Bas agreed thickly. 'But my bitter hatred for him was. You taught me to love instead. You showed me how to listen. And how to forgive.'

'You have forgiven your brother?' She could scarcely believe it.

It felt too good to be real.

'We have a way to go,' he admitted. 'But we're getting there. Though it turns out he didn't really need forgiveness.'

'No?'

'No,' Bas confirmed. 'Rather he sacrificed more than I knew. *For* me. And if it hadn't been for you, I would never have known that. I would have carried around that weighty, debilitating burden for the rest of my life. You've given me chance to become a different man. A *better* man. You've given me back my relationship with my brother.'

That warmth in her chest had swelled so much that she thought it might spill out everywhere.

This was the Basilius she had always thought lurked beneath that suave exterior and naughty reputation. She wasn't sure she had really believed she would ever see it, though.

She certainly hadn't imagined that she would have anything to do with it.

'You did that yourself.' She couldn't keep the

smile from her lips, even as the prickling in her eyes finally spilled over.

He didn't answer. He merely reached out his arms and pulled her to him, his lips pressed to the top of her head.

'You're the only one for me, Naomi,' he muttered. 'How could I ever have thought different? My life is nothing without you in it. You, and our baby.'

'I feel the same,' she murmured, her hand moving to cup his face. His jaw sitting squarely in the softness of her palm.

'I already strong-armed you into moving in with me,' he told her. 'And then agreeing to marry me. But, now, I think it's time I asked you. Properly.'

She opened her mouth ready to agree, but then he opened the box and she could only stare at the ring in front of her. Five stones winked back at her, three diamonds and two stunning emeralds, which she could have testified were the exact colour of the gown she had worn for the gala.

It was as though Bas had taken the very essence of that first night and poured it into such an exquisite piece of jewellery. Along with his heart and soul.

'Will you accept all that I have, Naomi Fox?' he asked solemnly. 'And I promise you that I will spend each and every day making sure you never live to regret that decision.'

It was everything she could have imagined. And more. The romantic notion she'd told him she didn't need, but it turned out that she thoroughly wanted.

As though he understood her better than she understood herself.

She offered a wry smile. It turned out he had a few lessons of his own that he wanted to teach *her*.

And she found she liked that. Very much.

'You've tattooed my name on your heart. I was half a man before I met you. I'd still be half a man now, if it hadn't been for you. I love you, Naomi. I think I fell in love with you that first night—I just couldn't have believed love existed for me. But we're a family. We were always meant to be. Come home with me, and promise me you'll never leave again.'

He was so earnest. Almost as though a part of him actually doubted she would agree. Did he really not know that she couldn't have denied him even if she'd wanted?

'I promise,' she choked out. 'You've given me everything I could ever have wanted. I love you, too, Bas. I always will.'

She watched as he slid the ring out of the box and onto her finger. Finally claiming her as his. The way she hadn't even allowed herself to dream it could be. Moments later, he stood back up and swept her into his embrace, before dipping his mouth to hers, to seal their promise.

The three of them already a little family.

For ever.

Finally.

* * * * *

*Look out for the next story in the
Billionaire Twin Surgeons duet*

Forbidden Nights with the Surgeon

*If you enjoyed this story, check out
these other great reads from
Charlotte Hawkes*

Tempted by Her Convenient Husband
Reunited with His Long-Lost Nurse
The Doctor's One Night to Remember

All available now!